THE RED CHURCH

THE CRANE DIARIES 4

BY APRYL BAKER

THE RED CHURCH

Limitless Publishing, LLC
Kailua, HI 96734
www.limitlesspublishing.com

Formatting: Limitless Publishing

ISBN-13: 978-1-64034-836-3
ISBN-10: 1-64034-836-0

DEDICATION

For Alisha Vincent

1

"Pay attention!"

I come awake with a start, blinking at my grandmother. Lila Crane is not a woman to be trifled with, but I can't help it. She's trying to help me memorize all the people I need to know for my dad's big charity ball this weekend, something I'm not looking forward to. It'll be a room full of rich people, and the wealthy and I don't mix well.

"I swear, Emma, it's like you don't even care. This is important to your father."

"I'm sorry," I mutter and sit up. Row after row of pictures are splayed out on the dining room table with index cards beside each one with all the pertinent information about the individual. "I don't know why we're even doing this. You know I'm not going to remember a single name."

"Certainly not if you can't even stay awake long enough to learn them." Lila sounds as fed up as I am, but hey, I never asked for this. It was all her idea. She wrangled me into it.

"Do I really have to know all these people? I'm never going to see them again after the party."

"Yes, you will be seeing them again." Lila taps her fingers impatiently on the dining room table. "These people are ones your father has strong ties to, ones who donate quite a bit to his charity to feed the poor, but more importantly, some of them are Ezekiel's friends. They've been waiting to meet you since he brought you home."

Gee, think she could put even more pressure on me?

"*Grandmère*, I get that it's important..."

"Do you?" Lila's blue gaze is like a

laser as she pins me with it. "Because if you did, I think you'd put a little more effort into learning the names of the people who are important to your father."

"*Je déteste ça*," I mutter under my breath.

"And you don't think I hate having to sit here and force you to do something you clearly have no interest in?" she asks, exasperated. "At least your French is getting better."

"It's why I took a French language class." I rub my eyes, tired. "Everyone was getting frustrated with my lack of knowledge, and I didn't want to embarrass you."

"Embarrass me?" Lila stops her fingernail tapping. "You could never embarrass me, your *grandpère*, or your papa."

I look pointedly at the pictures. "Isn't that the point of this? So I won't embarrass you all?"

"Of course not. We just want you to be prepared…" She trails off, her eyes going wide. "Oh, my. I never thought…Emma, we are not embarrassed by you."

They may all say that, but deep in their hearts, they are. They're rich, and they travel in all the right circles. My manners are not on par with theirs, and I've seen Lila wince on more than one occasion when we were talking with her friends and I said something that was more blunder than actual conversation.

"This isn't me, *Grandmère*. It will never be me, and I feel like I let you down at every turn because of it. I'm a jeans and t-shirt kind of girl. I'd rather get Taco Bell and binge something on Netflix than go to a charity ball. I'm sorry I'm not the girl who loves parties and shopping and dining out at fancy restaurants. I wish you had that girl instead of me, but I am who I am, and trying to make me be that other girl is only making me miserable."

Wow, I can't believe I said that. Neither can Lila, from the look on her face.

"Here's my beautiful girl." My grandfather, Josiah, waltzes into the room in his standard polo shirt and cargo shorts. Lila hates him wearing this particular outfit, but in New Orleans, between the heat and the humidity, the less clothes, the better. Or thin fabric at a minimum.

"Hey, Grandpa." I grin at him, grateful he's way less formal than Lila, who insists on being called the French word for grandmother. "Is Papa with you?" The two of them flew out to California a few days ago on business. I knew they were coming back today, but I wasn't sure of what time

"No. He went home. Said something about a date with Nancy."

Nancy Moriarity was my old social worker back in Charlotte, North Carolina. I'm glad she moved down here shortly after I did. She's the closest thing I have to a real mother, and with her dating my dad, I have really high hopes he'll make her my stepmother.

Lila makes a face, and my protective instincts rise. "Something wrong with Nancy?"

"No, of course not. She's just not who your father usually dates."

"Is it because she's black?" The Cranes

come from old money, and as such, they have serious social handicaps.

"Don't be ridiculous. Nancy could be green and from Saturn, for all I care. I was simply stating a fact. Your father tends to date women who come from the same..."

"The same what?" I narrow my eyes, trying to hold my temper in check. "You think less of Nancy because her bank account isn't as big as yours? Or is it that she works with the poor and gets down into the trenches with them to pull them out?"

Lila's mouth opens and closes, clearly not expecting my outburst or my hostility. That makes two of us. I'm in a mood today, and I don't know why.

Josiah puts his arm around me. "Your *grandmère* means no harm, sweetheart. Nancy is the first woman your father's dated who hasn't been overly wealthy, but we don't hold that against her. It's a shock to us, that's all. We like Nancy just fine."

Leave it to Josiah to play peacemaker. I can't help how defensive of Nancy I am. I wouldn't be standing here today if not for her.

"Neither of you understand what Nancy did for me. Do you know how many foster kids end up in jail, on drugs, or dead within ninety days of being dumped out of the system with no one there to support them? Over half of them. That's where I would have been if not for Nancy. She always checked on me, gave me flack when my grades were bad, but more than anything, she stayed when everyone else left. When I pushed her away, Nancy kept coming back. She made me realize I was going down a bad path, helped me get myself together. I wasn't going to be a statistic. I already had grades good enough for a scholarship when Zeke and you guys came into my life. All because of Nancy. She loves me, but more than that, she never walked away from me. When anyone tries to tear her down or think less of her, I'm going to hit back. Hard."

Both my grandparents stare at me, dumbstruck. Leave it to me to silence the room. It seems to be all I do these days.

"I have to go. I'm supposed to meet Mary and Eric. I'll see you later."

"Emma, wait..." Lila calls after me, but I ignore her and head out to my car. I don't have the emotional energy to deal with her right now. I'm spiraling, and I don't know how to stop myself. Ever since I healed Dan last month, it's like I can't get control of my emotions. They're a hot mess, which, in turn, makes me a hot mess.

I do have to meet Mary and Eric, but not until later. They want us to discuss the first episode of our YouTube series. We're still arguing over the name of the show. Mary wants it simple, while Eric wants it to be weird and something people will remember. Me? I couldn't care less since I really don't want to do it, but my sister is a force of nature when it comes to getting what she wants.

My phone rings, and I glance at the screen to see Cass Willow's name pop up. I use the car's Bluetooth system to answer it.

"Hey, stranger. I haven't heard from you since I got back from Charlotte."

"Well, you been gettin' dat man of yours all settled in, *chèr*."

Cass's deep Cajun accent is charming. Mary calls it panty melting charming, but I don't see it. Maybe because I love my boyfriend. Dan is all I want. Cass does nothing for me. He's gorgeous, mind you, and if I wasn't in love with my boyfriend, I might go there. But as it is, he's more like a surrogate brother.

"Let's not talk about Dan. The police department has been keeping him so busy, I barely see him."

Which is another reason I'm in such an awful mood. I miss Dan. He had to stay in the hospital for a week after his mother shot him and tried to kill us both. His soul is tied to mine, and if he dies, theoretically, so should I, but I have doubts about that now. He and his dad moved down here two weeks ago, and I might have seen him three times since them. Lots of texts and video chatting, but it's not the same.

"You up for a little huntin', den, *chèr*?"

Cass Willow is a hunter, as is his entire

9

family. They don't just track down ghosts who have gone mad. A hunter deals with all brands of the supernatural.

"What kind of hunting?"

"I'm no' sure yet. A friend of de family asked us to go and walk dere property. Kasey is supposed to meet us dere, and I t'ought if you weren' busy, you migh' want to come and help out?"

"Who's Kasey?"

"He owns de place."

"What kind of problems?"

"It's a long story. I'll fill you in when we get dere."

"Why not? It'll keep me out of Mary and Eric's clutches for a little while longer."

"Dey still tryin' to get you to do dere show?"

"There is no trying to it. They've got it all set up, right down to the first episode. They just can't agree on the title for the show."

Cass laughs. "Good luck wit' dat. I'll text you de address."

Once Cass hangs up, his text comes right through, and I program it into the

GPS. It's not far from here, which means it's probably more rich people and their snobby hang-ups. Not what I need today, but they deserve help as much as the next person when it comes to the supernatural wrecking their lives.

Pulling out of the drive, I leave my problems with Lila behind and try to focus on what I can do. Help someone.

The house is about ten minutes outside the city, which gives me the chance to look at all the Christmas decorations going up in and around New Orleans. Bourbon Street is a place I really want to check out, but I promised Mary and Eric we'd all go together when Dan has a night off. It's a street full of bars, and I'm curious to see what kind of decorations they put up.

My grandparents live in their townhome in the Garden District, and as such, their decorations are tasteful, if a little boring. I much prefer the way Mary and I decorated our dorm room with strands of twinkling multi-colored lights, a Christmas tree that is bigger than the room allows, and all kinds of crazy knick-knacks. I swear, it looks like the elves from Santa's workshop threw up in there, but I love it.

The closer I get to my destination, the sparser the houses get. Lots of people didn't rebuild after Hurricane Katrina, and that's sad to me. I can understand their need to escape a place full of such tragedy, but some of these homes could really be fixed up and sold, helping to rebuild the community. It gives me an idea for helping to fund my special project, but I'll talk to Zeke about it later.

My GPS lets me know I've arrived at the location. To the right is a gated property, and I pull up to it. Rolling down my window, I hit the button to alert the house I'm here, but there's no reply. After several attempts—hey, it's just like an elevator button to me—I give up and decide to wait for Cass.

Getting out of the car, I move so I can see the house. It's obscured by the trees leading up the driveway. Well, dang. Leave it to Cass to send me to an empty house I have no way of getting into. Even I can't pick an electronic lock. Yet.

"Hello, there."

Startled at the sound of a voice, I turn to see a man sitting on a fallen log to the side of the gate. How I missed him, I have no idea, but there he is. He's tall, with dark brown hair and green eyes. Older than I am, maybe. He could be twenty-five or forty-five. He has one of those ageless faces, but that doesn't make him any less handsome. He's wearing light gray slacks and a loose linen dress shirt with the sleeves rolled up. His accent is definitely local, but more like Lila's. Cultured and genteel. French Creole. Old money. Maybe he owns the place.

"Are you Kasey?"

"No. I'm Simon Ayers."

"So you're not the owner of the house?" Then what's he doing sitting out here all by himself with no car? I stare harder, trying to discern if he's a wandering spirit set free from his body, but he feels flesh and blood to me.

"*Mais*, no. I was out of town when they

14

auctioned off the property."

"Then what are you doing here without a car?"

"I was hoping to catch the owner. I'd heard he was having some construction done. I want to try to buy the property from him, but he's not here, as you can see. Since I'm technically on my lunch hour, I asked my driver to leave me here. I like the area, and it gave me an excuse to get out of the office. I hate the boardroom."

"Me too," I mutter.

He quirks a brow. "You don't look old enough to be in a boardroom."

"I'm Emma Crane."

His eyes widen slightly. "You're a little famous around these parts."

Don't I know it. I'm the girl who was kidnapped and found years later. Everywhere I go, I get recognized, and it wears a person down. I came here for a fresh start and to escape people knowing who I am and what I can do, but that's not what happened. I've gone from one frying pan into another.

I've even had a few cameras shoved in

my face. I think all the local paparazzi got a bit more cautious after that little incident.

"I don't want to be famous."

He smiles wryly. "Be that as it may, as Ezekiel Crane's only child, you're going to be in the spotlight. Don't let it get to you. Use it to your advantage instead."

It's my turn to quirk a brow. Who is this guy?

"I inherited the business when my father passed. I was the black sheep of the family, spending all my time carousing in Europe instead of here helping out. When I came back, there was some very unkind whispering going around the social circles. I had a bit of notoriety myself, albeit not like yours, but I turned that into success. I used my notoriety to get people involved and strengthened the business because of it. If you can find a way to do that, then let them talk all they want."

I kinda like him. He's not stuffy, and he doesn't appear to be as snobby as I'd dubbed most rich people.

"It's nice to meet you."

"You as well, Emma Crane."

"Do you know anything about the history of the property?"

"Of course. It's a piece I want to add to my collection."

"Your collection?"

"I collect unusual and strange things. This place fits nicely into that, even though it's a little morbid."

Morbid?

"Do you know the history of *La Nouvelle-Orléans*?"

"Not really. I didn't grow up here."

"*La Nouvelle-Orléans*, or New Orleans as most call it, was founded in 1718 by Jean-Baptiste Le Moyne de Bienville who worked for the French Mississippi Company. This place was built as an abbey in 1719 right after the French claimed it. They wanted to bring aid and refuge to the inhabitants. It remained an abbey until 1822, well after the city became a part of the United States with the Louisiana Purchase in 1803."

They are all very boring facts, but he has a storyteller's voice, much like the spook doctor and my uncle, Lawrence

Olivet.

"To the locals, it's called The Red Church."

"The Red Church?" I glanced toward the building that is barely visible. I thought it was a house, not a church. All I can make out is a lot of stone. "That doesn't sound like a cool nickname."

"It's not. This place is steeped in tragedy and blood. During the War of 1812, a massacre happened here. All of the sisters and the priests were murdered in quite a brutal fashion. Some say it was the British, but others think it was something else altogether."

"Something else?"

"You are your father's daughter, so *oui*, something else." He grins lazily. "It was never proven, though, and the Vatican decided to reopen the abbey. Only strange things began to occur. As to what those strange things were, it's not widely known. It's said the Vatican has the journals of all who lived here over the next ten years, and those journals describe what occurred within the walls. The church finally closed it when all the sisters hung themselves on Christmas Eve in 1822."

"They hung themselves?"

He nods, his eyes becoming troubled. "*Oui*. It is why I believe this ground is cursed. Perhaps it was cursed before the abbey was built, or perhaps it happened with the deaths of those poor souls in 1812. I can't be sure, but I do know this place is not fit for anyone to live here, and that is what I fear this new owner plans on doing. The abbey comes with over twenty acres of land. One could easily build a housing or commercial development here. It's why I'm determined to buy it."

"For a guy who spent years bouncing around Europe, you don't sound like a black sheep of any family. You sound responsible."

He throws his head back and laughs. He has this nice, easy, rich laugh. I smile despite myself.

"*Mais*, but you are a treasure, Emma Crane. No one, not even the people who work for me, would ever call me responsible. I get up to all sorts of dastardly deeds."

"And you talk like someone out of the nineteenth century."

"My mother's doing. We were all taught proper English and attended a private school that fostered that as well."

"What got you interested in the supernatural?"

"I'm from New Orleans, *chèr*." He winks. "Everyone around here knows about the supernatural."

"There's a difference between knowing and *knowing*."

"True," he agrees. "But all the natives, no matter their socio-economic class, know about the supernatural. Even the ones who try to pretend they don't know it's as real as you and me. Deep in their bones, they feel the pull of the Loa, the spirits."

He's right about that. Most people don't want to know the truth. It's easier to believe the scary things you see on TV or read about in books aren't real, that they can't get you. I wish sometimes I didn't know about them. I'd be a lot saner than I am.

"Now, Miss Emma, since I've answered your questions, will you answer some of mine?"

I shrug. "Sure."

"What are *you* doing out here?"

"I'm meeting the owner and a friend of mine, Cass Willow."

"You know the young hunter?"

"You know he's a hunter?"

He smiled. "*Oui*. You don't collect the things I have without running into a few hunters here and there. Cass and his family are well known in these parts. I've taken a few dangerous items his family has come across and stored them in a vault where they can no longer harm anyone."

Speak of the devil, and so shall he appear.

Cass's old beat up Ford Mustang rolls to a halt behind my own Lexus. He and his cousins, Caryle and Robert, exit the car. Cass looks surprised to see Simon here, but the grin that breaks out across his face tells me more than anything Simon could have about his trustworthiness. If Cass trusts him, then I guess I can too. At least to a point.

The way he spoke about his "collection" bothered me. I'm not sure why, but it did. He had this look in his eyes that I can't define. I make a note to ask Cass about him later.

"Simon, wha' are you doing here?"

Cass has this really thick Cajun accent he only lets out around people he knows well. I noticed it when I first met him. The more he got to know me, the thicker it became. When he's around anyone new, it's barely detectable. I'm not sure why he does that. His accent is quite charming.

"I wanted to get a look at the property and meet the new owner. I'm hoping he'll sell it to me."

Cass's eyes stray to the locked gate. "He wants to develop it, but every single crew he's brought in has up and quit on him."

"And how did he know to call you?" I ask.

Cass shrugs. "We helped out his general contractor wit' a bit of boogeyman problem."

Boogeyman? The boogeyman is real? I shake my head at the absurdity of it, but with what I've seen, of course the boogeyman would be real.

"Emma!" Caryle throws her arms around me, and I stagger back under the weight of it, a little shocked. I'm not really a huggy-feeley kind of girl outside of my family.

"Caryle, leave de girl alone." Robert disentangles his sister from me. "Sorry, she be in one of her I-need-to-hug-everyone moods."

Robert, Caryle, and Cass all look alike with their dirty blond hair. Caryle and her brother have brown eyes, whereas Cass's are blue. You'd think they were brothers and sister if you didn't know better. Cass's family was murdered by a Rougarou when he was little, though, and his aunt and uncle raised him after that. They taught him to be a hunter.

"What?" Caryle pouts. "I haven't seen her in forever."

"You saw her over de weekend." Robert rolls his eyes.

"Like I said, forever!" Caryle flips her

long blonde hair over her shoulder and flashes her brother a grin. At sixteen, she's a handful. God help us all when she graduates and gets out on her own. We'll spend all our time putting out fires. The girl is trouble without even trying. Not that she means to be trouble. She just doesn't think things through before jumping in.

A lot like me at that age, only way nicer. There isn't a mean bone in her body.

"Emma." Cass turns that wicked grin of his on me. "T'ank you for comin', *chèr*."

"I had nothing else going on." And it got me away from my grandparents for a while. I needed a break.

"Has Simon filled you in on de history of de property?"

I nod. "He has. It sounds gruesome."

"You doan know de half of it." Cass pulls out a piece of paper and walks up to the gate. He punches in the electronic code, and the gate swings open. "But you will soon enough."

Instead of driving up to the old church,

we walk. Simon invites himself along, and none of the Willows seem to mind. He really does know them well.

Feeling a little uneasy, I fall into step with Caryle and follow them up to The Red Church.

It certainly doesn't look like a red church.

The stone is old and stained, but it has character. That's what I notice first. Not the overgrown weeds or the cemetery off to the side full of cracked headstones. Not the ground that feels soft beneath our feet even though it hasn't rained in weeks. It is the stone building itself that holds my attention. It's the artist in me.

The church reminds me of the older churches in town. An arched doorway leads into the main building, a single window sitting above the archway beneath the A-line roof. A second wing spreads out behind the main church, giving it depth and width. Long windows line the building on both sides, with doorways at each end of the second wing under the same rooftop. The arched dome that sits between the sections of the church with a large cross sitting on its roof is what captures me. It gives the building majesty and more than a little mystery. It's gorgeous.

The building and surrounding area, including the cemetery, is shrouded in a fine mist. Which is odd because the day is clear. Not even a whisper of rain in the air, but here, there's not so much as a ray of sunshine cutting through the thick layer of fog.

I slow and fall behind the others, feeling something reach out toward me— a caress, almost.

Something I've never felt before. It's not good, and it's not evil. It just…is.

"Emma?" Cass calls, but I ignore him and turn in a circle, trying to figure out where this feeling is coming from.

It reminds me of a ghost's energy, but it feels bigger than that, more intense.

"Robert, take dem on up to de church.

Emma and I will be along in a minute."

"Do you feel it?" I whisper when he comes to a stop beside me.

"I feel som'tin." A shiver rolls through him. "Not sure wha', dou."

"It's not a ghost. It's more than that. It's…"

Closing my eyes, I try to reach for it, but it shies away from me, staying at the very edge of my senses. I take a few steps forward, and the thing, whatever it is, tries to push me back.

It doesn't want me going near that church.

"It feels like som'tin is tryin' to stop me from moving forward." Cass wraps his arms around himself. "I doan want to go in dere, but we have to. Dis, whatever it is, it's tryin' to stop us."

Maybe Cass is more sensitive than I thought. Not as human as he thinks he is. Or maybe he's a little psychic and just feels the strangeness around him. Or maybe he's become so accustomed to hunting these things, his mind has adapted and learned. The maybes can go on forever. I'll have a talk with Zeke. He might have the answers since he works with so many who feel the supernatural on a regular basis.

The presence presses in closer, and I take a step back. Cass does as well. Whatever this thing is, it's strong.

I can taste it on my tongue. Bitter honey that's slightly burnt. Several deep breaths later, and the scent is so thick around me, it's all I can smell.

"It's the Loa."

Cass and I both jump when Simon speaks. He's a sneaky devil. Not good for my health. Ghosts are bad enough about getting the jump on me. I don't need humans doing it too.

"Don't do that."

He grins unabashedly. "I told you I'm known for my dastardly deeds, and that includes scaring poor, innocent, young ladies."

Cass groans. "Doan get him started. He'll go on and on in dat old English forever."

"Please. You know you've picked up a few things from me that have helped you with the ladies."

Cass narrows his eyes, but I put a stop to the argument before it begins. "You said it's the Loa? The voodoo spirits?"

The smile dies from Simon's lips. "*Oui*. They don't want us here."

"It does feel like something pushing at me, trying to force me to go back. Cass feels it too."

"They've taken a liking to you both, then." Simon nods toward where Caryle and her brother are waiting by the church door. Neither of them looks the least bit uncomfortable.

"Do you feel it too?"

Simon nods. "I wish I didn't. Once the Loa take a liking to you, they can call on you. Make you do things."

"Not me. I don't do anything I don't want to."

Simon looks like he wants to say something, but Cass shakes his head. "*Non*, Simon, she be tellin' you true. She doan do any'tin she doan woan to. Beings far more powerful den de Loa have tried and failed."

Whispering surrounds us when Cass makes that statement. They're close,

close enough to reach out and touch, but I shrink away from them. They're angry.

"I think we'd best get inside, Cass." They're angry enough to hurt him, and I instinctively know they can.

His eyes narrow, and he turns his head, looking out over the gray fog that is rolling in thicker and thicker.

"Doan be worried about me, *chèr*. Dey cain't hurt me ei'der." He holds up his hand, and I see a bracelet wrapped around it. "Dis gris gris, it protects me from de Loa. I piss 'em off more den anyone I know."

"That sounds about right." I laugh and sling an arm around him, leaning into him. Cass has quickly turned into one of my best friends. Maybe it's because he reminds me of Eli. I don't know, but I do know I'll protect him at any cost.

I push that thought out to the whispers surrounding us, letting them know I will hurt them if they try to hurt him.

I don't know if they believe me, and I don't wait to find out. We quickly walk up the dirt path to where Caryle and Robert wait.

"Took you long enough." Caryle pushes off the wall. "What were you doing, anyway?"

"Sightseeing," I say wryly. "Why didn't you go inside?"

"By ourselves?" Caryle looks horrified at the thought.

"Aren't you hunters?"

Caryle laughs, outright laughs. "Sure are, sugar, but we ain't dumb hunters. We be smarter den dat."

Caryle always works to keep her Cajun accent in check. It's rare when it slips out, but when it does, it serves to remind you that she's not your typical sixteen-year-old girl. She's a hunter, and she's as dangerous as any of the rest of us. Human, yes, but still dangerous. Whereas Cass's accent is charming, Caryle's is lethal. Maybe that's why she doesn't use it.

"Shouldn't the owner be here by now?" I glance to Cass, who's chuckling at his cousin.

"He's running late. He gave me the access code to get inside the gate. The church isn't locked."

"No?" I tilt my head and study the structure. "I'd lock it."

"The abbey has never once been locked, not since it was built. It was a tradition, and one the inhabitants of the area honored even when the Vatican pulled its support." Simon comes to stand next to me, gesturing to the entrance. "New Orleans is big on tradition, especially its religious traditions."

He's right about that. New Orleans is a melting pot of traditions, but to the people here, it doesn't matter. They pay homage to them all.

Cass slides his arm around me and pulls me away from Simon. "Come on, Emma, let's go have a look around."

I cast him a questioning look but don't comment. His expression is unreadable. I'll ask him what that was all about later. Right now, I'm too curious about the church.

The inside is in just as much disrepair as the outside, which is a shame. It's beautiful. The architecture is amazing, right out of the eighteenth century. Since moving to New Orleans, I've become obsessed with the architecture, so much so I've even changed my major to architectural engineering. I want to be able to build the things I draw.

It's barren aside from a few broken bits of wood that might once have been pews. The stone is stained dark brown in places, and I wonder if that's where some of the priests and nuns were killed during the massacre. It certainly could have been, but it could have been the blood of vagrants as well.

"It's beautiful." My eyes sweep the walls, the broken stained-glass windows, and the stone floors. This place could easily be converted to a home or rebuilt as a parish church.

"You think so?" Caryle's nose scrunches up. "I think it's creepy."

"You have to look past the creepy." I slip out of Cass's grasp and walk deeper into the church, toward the back where the walls branch out and become wider. "This place is full of beauty. Even steeped in death and blood, it's beautiful."

"She's impressive," I hear Simon tell

Cass.

"She's got a boyfriend who would put you down in seconds." The hard rebuke in Cass's voice is enough to make me turn and look at them.

"Cass?"

He shakes his head. "Just lettin' Simon know you're taken, dat's all."

"I wasn't…"

Cass cuts Simon off. "She be off limits, Simon."

I arch a brow at him. "I can speak for myself, you know."

"I know." A small grin finally tugs at the corners of his mouth. "Trust me, Emma, I know."

I turn my attention back to Simon. He's standing there, smiling. Something about him is off. I like him well enough, but I don't trust him. Part of it's my own inability to trust people because I grew up in the foster care system. Part of it is my instincts telling me there's something dark in Simon, no matter how much good he does. Either way, he needs to understand I really am off limits.

"Cass is right. I do have a boyfriend,

and I'm not looking to replace him."

"Perhaps in the future, then." Simon winks at me, and my stomach sours.

"No. Dan is it for me. There will never be anyone else."

"You're young yet, *ma chèr*," Simon says. "Things happen, people change."

"I'm not nearly as young as you think I am." Not emotionally, not mentally, and certainly not metaphysically, but he doesn't need to know that. "Now, let's get back to the situation at hand. Cass, tell me what's been going on here to warrant a hunter's touch."

"Well, aside from de history of de place, I doan know. I was asked to meet Kasey here. We were referred."

"Okay, tell me about the guy who referred you. You said he was a construction foreman or something? Can we talk to him?"

"Sure can, darlin', but first we need to be speakin' wit' de owner. He should be here soon enough."

People who are late irritate me. I guess it comes from me trying my best to be on time. Working with Zeke has also given me an appreciation for things getting done in a timely manner. I don't want to be a part of his business, but he was right that it makes sense for me to learn a little about it. Should something ever happen to him, the entire organization goes to me. His company is not publicly traded. It belongs to the Crane family, and the Cranes alone. There is no board of directors. All decisions are made by my father. Sure, he has a group of advisors who basically fill the role of a board, but they don't have the power a normal board has. Only Zeke and Josiah have that power.

It still amazes me that the company is as big as it is without going public. I understand the reasons behind them not doing it, though. Some of the things they do aren't quite legal, and a board could potentially do something about that. Zeke needs it structured the way it is. I'm not exactly above doing illegal things myself, so I don't judge. Much to Dan's horror. My boyfriend is a police detective, and my dad makes him uncomfortable. But Zeke respects Dan and doesn't hold his job against him.

"We should probably look around, then." I glance at Simon and frown. I don't want him seeing what I can do. I don't share my abilities with strangers.

"Robert, why doan you and Caryle take Simon outside and check out de graveyard?"

Caryle starts to argue, but Robert interrupts her. "Sure. Is dere any'tin we should look for?"

"Just keep your eyes open."

Robert nods and steers his sister toward the door. Simon hasn't moved.

"I think I'd rather look around in here," Simon says after a moment.

Then I won't be using my gifts. "Sure. You can come along if you want to."

Cass's lips thin, but he doesn't argue. He knows me well enough to know I'll come back later and do my thing.

Once Robert and Caryle have gone, we start forward. There's a door that leads into the back hallway between the extension and the front of the church. A large spiral staircase sits in the middle of the hallway. It must lead to the circular structure I admired so much.

That's where I go first. The hallway at the top of the stairs is a circle with three doors and a window overlooking the front of the church and the surrounding area. You could see for miles up here.

"I could sit here for hours and just draw."

"*Non, chèr*, you doan want to be doin' dat." Cass gently pulls me away from the window. "Dis place, dis is where all de nuns hanged demselves. Bad juju."

I keep my reaper abilities firmly locked down, but I do look around. The air up here isn't cold. It's warm. With it being December, it's not as hot as it is in the summer, but it's not cold either. You don't need a jacket during the day. If there was a ghost around, the place would be icy.

"You're wondering why it isn't cold?" Simon leans against a wall and watches us.

"Usually, if a place is haunted, it's cold."

He nods. "Usually."

"I hear a but in dere." Cass tilts his

head and studies Simon, his eyes assessing.

"But I think whatever stalks these halls knows we're here to hunt it, and it's hiding. It's making all the ghosts here hide as well."

"Crafty little beast." That actually makes sense. Ghosts can hide from me, but not for long. Eventually, they're drawn to the reaper's light inside of me. Kane, my reaping tutor, tells me I shine as bright as a lighthouse beacon. Eric told me that once while he was still a ghost. Ghosts can't help but be drawn to it. I have the ability to help them cross over, and they instinctively want that, even if they don't know it.

Cass nods and opens the door he's standing next to and walks in. I follow him, Simon right on our heels. It's a bedroom, or at least what's left of one. The bed frame is broken, lying in pieces on the floor, the mattress long gone. An old dresser sits against one wall. That's it for the furniture. But the floor is covered in debris, used needles, and it stinks to high heaven. Like old piss and throw up.

"Careful of the needles," Cass warns.

Since I have no desire to catch something, I'm more than careful of where I step. This room is slightly colder than anywhere else. I don't think Cass or Simon notices the difference, but I do. I'm more attuned to the energy that makes up a ghost, though. Something's in here. I can't pinpoint where, exactly, but it's here. The cold was my first clue, but the more I stand here, the more I can feel it. It's watching us.

I don't think it's the big bad Simon believes haunts these halls, but it's a ghost. Good or bad, I don't know. I call for Kane, keeping my back to both Simon and Cass. Neither of them will see him. He only shows himself to humans if he wants to, and I don't need to speak aloud to him. We can communicate in our heads.

Kane appears almost instantly. He must not have been doing anything. He's dressed in his normal jeans and a green t-shirt, his shaggy black hair a mess. Green eyes look questioningly at me.

They can't know you're here, I tell

him.

What are you doing here, Emma? This is a bad place to be.

Cass asked me to come along and walk the property. He's been retained to deal with whatever's here.

None of you should be here. It's too dangerous.

"Em, you okay?"

"Fine, Cass. Just thinking, imagining what the room might have looked like before. It's the artist in me. I can't help it."

Kane snorts at my lie. Lies come easily to me. I'm a born liar. I make no apologies for it either.

"You and your drawin'." He shakes his head. "Come on, girl. Let's see wha's in de o'der rooms."

See if you can figure out who's hiding in here, I tell Kane as I follow Cass out of the rooms. He nods and turns to face the room. He'll figure out who's in there, so I don't worry about it.

The other two rooms are more bedrooms, similar to the one we'd left, so we waste no more time up here and go back downstairs. The next room we come to is a kitchen of sorts. There are old tables and counters. Three large fireplaces take up one entire wall. They would have used the spits built into the structure to cook with as well as the large area around where the fire was built in the hollowed-out bottom.

How people used fire to cook with is beyond me. Eric wants us to go camping, but Mary and I keep putting him off. We enjoy the outdoors, not the woods. We aren't camping girls. We're more "let's hike for a mile then collapse in the hotel room."

A spacious dining hall is off the kitchen, with a small hallway that leads back to the front room, which is where the actual church must have been. We go back out into the main hallway and turn right instead of left this time.

Large rooms full of beds line one wall. The sleeping quarters for the nuns. I'm assuming the head nun had one of the upstairs rooms, as well as the priest. The other wall holds a library. Old books line the falling-down shelves, some of them rotting due to the exposure to the elements. None of the windows in the entire building survived. Even the stained-glass ones are broken. Some are jagged pieces, some completely broken out, and some just have holes in the glass.

"That is a disgrace." Simon walks over to the bookshelves and starts examining the books. "These would have been valuable, and no one thought to remove them before they were ruined." He shakes his head, disgusted.

I agree with him. Libraries are not my thing, but I understand the value of books. Books hold the knowledge we need to learn, to grow, to become more than we are, just as much as actual hands-on learning. I respect the written word a lot more than I used to.

Again, there is no temperature drop down here. The ghosts really are hiding. Maybe it's us, maybe it's the Loa outside that frighten them, but they're not coming out to play.

Cass tilts a brow at me while Simon is busy.

I shake my head, just as frustrated as

he is. Sure, this place would make a fantastic set for a horror movie because it is creepy, but it doesn't feel dangerous. Even the presence I felt up in the bedroom didn't cause alarm. It felt more sad and frightened than monstrous.

"Cass!"

We both turn when we hear Robert shouting.

"Yo?" Cass yells down the hallway.

"Kasey's here!"

Could Robert not have come found us instead of yelling? If there is something here, they might well have scared it back into its hiding place. As I said, ghosts eventually find me, and that's what I was banking on until the boys started screaming and potentially ruined it.

"Come on, let's go meet de owner and find out wha's been goin' on here."

At least now we might get an idea of what's been happening. The more information I have, the better I can deal with what's here. If there's anything here at all outside of a few scared ghosts.

Kasey Jones is not what I expected. He's standing in the middle of the room talking to Robert and Caryle. The man might be thirty, but I'm guessing he's closer to twenty-five or twenty-six. He has that almost teenager-ish look to him still. He's tall, taller than anyone in the room, and built. His blond hair has been bleached by many hours in the sun, his deep tan a testament to that, and his sky-blue eyes remind me of Mary's. He could be our age, for all I know.

I figured the owner would be some guy in his late forties or fifties. A man who would show up in a business suit as opposed to board shorts and a yellow tank top that reads "I don't do mornings."

"Hey." Kasey turns when he sees us come into the room. "Thanks for coming out."

He has no accent. None. He definitely isn't a New Orleans native.

"No problem." Cass steps forward and shakes his hand. His Cajun accent has disappeared as well. Him and strangers. "We're glad to help."

"I'm not sure there's anything to help with." Kasey shrugs and waves his arm at the interior of the church. "I think it's more of a case of superstitious people getting freaked out by the surroundings and the legends about this place."

"Do you believe in the supernatural?" I ask him.

"Not even a little. I think this is a waste of time. No offense to any of you."

"None taken." He reminds me of Dan in his quick denial. Dan came around even before he came into his own abilities, and I have a feeling Kasey will as well. "Simon tells us you want to commercialize the property?"

"Simon?" Kasey glances at the man.

"Simon Ayers." He steps forward and shakes Kasey's hand. "I'm hoping you'll sell the property to me. I'll give you top dollar for it."

"No, I'm not selling. This place has phenomenal potential, and I plan on seeing that through. I want to do a housing complex on one side and then commercialize the rest with businesses and perhaps a technology park. I have big plans for it."

"Perhaps you'll change your mind." Simon hands him a business card. "It's time for me to be going along. I do have a business to run, as the many texts messages have reminded me. My driver is out front." He turns to me and hands over a business card as well. "It was truly a pleasure to meet you, Miss Emma Crane." Fake tipping his hat, he turns and says goodbye to the others on his way out.

Something is off there, but I don't know what. Still, I like the guy. He might be a little off, but he's genuinely nice and not at all snobby. A big plus in my book.

"Kasey, you've met Caryle and Robert.

THE RED CHURCH

Allow me to introduce you to Emma Crane. She helps us out here and there."

"Crane?" Kasey frowns. "Any relation to Ezekiel Crane?"

"He's my father."

Kasey smiles. "He wants to invest in the property here if I can get people to stay on the job."

"Papa does love his real estate investments, and he never invests in something he doesn't believe will earn him a potentially huge profit."

"That's what I'm hoping for too." He winks, his demeanor so much like Eric's I have to smile.

"How did you get into this business, anyway?" Caryle asks. "You don't look old enough to be in business."

"Caryle." Robert looks mortified, but Kasey only laughs.

"No worries. She's right. I'm only twenty-four, but I know more about the flipping business than most. My dad did it for a living, and I worked side by side with him since I was old enough to hold a hammer. I inherited some money from my grandmother when she died, so I

49

invested it in a house, and my dad helped me flip it. Since then, I've been flipping full time."

"You're not flipping this property, though?"

He shakes his head. "No. Like I said, I see the potential here, and I want a home base of operations. New Orleans has so many rundown and abandoned homes, it's a flipper's dream. I saw that last year when I was vacationing. I talked it over with my dad, and he agreed. This place is perfect for me to step out of his shadow and do things on my own. I have two ongoing flips here now, but this property is the one giving me trouble. I need workers here, and if you guys come in, do your thing, and tell them it's safe, then hopefully that'll be the end of it."

"Has Cass talked to you about the fee?"

"Fee?" Kasey frowns.

"You don't think we do this for free, do you?" I ignore Cass's frown. "There is a cost involved. Between time, cameras, our computer equipment, and any potential danger, it's not cheap."

"Danger?" Kasey smiles.

"Yes, Mr. Jones, I understand you don't believe in the supernatural, and that's fine, but I'm also referring to the vagrants who use this place to sleep. Some of them are quite dangerous. One stabbed Robert not two weeks ago. Almost nicked his kidney, so yes, there is danger involved."

"Huh. I never thought about that. What's the price?"

"It depends on how long it takes us to clear the place. A job typically runs three days minimum but can go longer. The standard fee is five thousand dollars, and depending on what happens and if we need to bring in more security or more equipment, it can run higher."

"Five grand?" His mouth drops open. "That's a little steep, don't you think?"

"What's more important to you? A little cash or getting your project back on schedule? The more time you lose, the more money you lose. As Papa likes to say, time is money."

He frowns, his brows diving down as he weighs my words.

"The locals know us," Cass pipes in. "If we say this place is clean, then they'll believe it."

"Blackmail," Kasey mutters, and I laugh.

"No, Mr. Jones, not at all. We're providing a service. And we will clean this place if possible."

"None of this is real, though."

"Just because you don't believe in it doesn't make it not real. It's as real as you and me, and trust me when I say it believes in you. And the people who work here. That's why it's dangerous. The more you believe in something, the more powerful it becomes, even if it's just in your own mind."

"You really believe in the supernatural?" Kasey's blue eyes are as open and honest as Dan's.

I nod. "I do. I've had up close and personal experiences. That's why I'm here. I help people."

"For a fee," he says ruefully.

"Only those who can afford it," I correct him. "That fee helps us help those who can't afford to move or hire people who can help them."

"And I can afford it." He laughs. "You are very much like your father, do you know that?"

"I do. So, what do you say, Mr. Jones? Do we have a deal?" I can feel the darkness that lives inside of me swell up. Demons make deals, and I try not to tap into my demonic side, but it always shines through at times. I make deals. Silas, my grandfather who is also a demon, encourages it. Which is why I try not to do it. It slips out sometimes, despite my best efforts.

"We have a deal, Miss Crane."

"Please call me Emma." I hold out my hand and shake his, sealing our deal. "I'll get the paperwork over to you later today."

I can feel the Willows staring holes through me, and I smile. They know about the creation of The Hathaway Foundation, but I doubt they know Dan's dad, Earl Richards, has already created the foundation and set up templates of all the various types of paperwork we'd need, including payment agreements for a job.

"Call me Kasey. Mr. Jones is my dad." His smile is genuine.

"Now, tell us what's been going on here that's caused every member of your crew to quit."

He sighs. "What *hasn't* happened is more apt of a question."

"What hasn't happened?"

"Work getting done, for one." He grins. "In all seriousness, I think the legends fed into their fears, and they started imaging things."

"Like what?" Caryle comes over and leans into me, eyeing Kasey like he's a piece of delicious candy.

"Like seeing nuns and priests walking the halls. Hearing footsteps and finding cold spots. I mean, I understand it gets a little chilly at night, but cold spots? It's as hot here as it is in California right now."

"Is that where you're from?"

He nods. "Born and raised in SoCal— Southern California."

Which explains his surfer boy vibe. He probably is a surfer.

"Did anything happen to any of the workers?"

Kasey nods, his expression turning serious. "Two of them fell down the stairs, claiming they were pushed. They were engineers trying to determine the best way to take the place down. I wanted to demolish it, but they wanted to see if anything of value could be saved and donated to the historical society."

"You can't tear this place down." I turn to face him, outraged. "It's too beautiful."

"Do you know how much it would cost to renovate it? To bring it up to code? There's not a stich of plumbing or wiring in the building."

"This building is a piece of our history here in New Orleans. It needs to be preserved." I stalk toward him. "Do you understand the historical significance? This building could be the center of your new development. The past meeting the present. It would make a perfect office for you and your base of operations."

"You're serious, aren't you?" Kasey looks around at the old stone walls that are stained with God only knows what.

"This church is beautiful. You *can't* tear it down."

"It's my property, and I can do what I want with it."

My eyes narrow. "And we don't have to help you, either."

"Blackmail again, even after we struck a handshake deal."

I snarl at him, my anger merging with my demonic side. "I'll blackmail you six ways to Sunday to save this place. If we don't cleanse it, no one in New Orleans will step foot in it. If you bring crews from outside the city, I guarantee you'll run into the same problems because, as I said before, just because you don't believe in something doesn't mean it's not real. The ghosts that haunt this land will ruin any potential profit you see before it can ever be realized."

He stares at me in amazement. "You can't be serious."

"I'm a Crane, Kasey, and I mean what I say."

His nostrils flare at the mention of my last name. He might think I'm crazy, but my last name holds sway. Most people in the real estate world know who my father is. He has his hand in all fifty states. Kasey knows my father can make or break him. He'll learn I can too.

"Fine. It's just a building."

"I'll have that stipulation included in our agreement I send over."

Surprise flickers in his eyes.

"As I said, I'm a Crane, and we aren't stupid either."

"Why is this place so important to you?"

"It just is." I can't explain why, but I knew it the minute I walked through the doors. This place needs to be saved.

"You're going to be a pain in my…"

"No cussing in a church."

He glares at me, but after a minute, a smile breaks free. "Want to have dinner with me?"

I blink at the unexpected question. "What?"

"A date, Emma. I'm asking you out on a date. So, what do you say? Will you have dinner with me?"

"I have a boyfriend."

"Da…dang."

At least he refrained from cussing.

"You and this boyfriend of yours, is it serious?"

"Dude." Robert slid over. "Her boyfriend is not someone you want to be pissing off."

"He a hunter too?"

"No. He's a police detective," I say, warning Robert with my eyes. No one needs to know about Dan's abilities and the fact that he carries the Sword of Truth, one of four holy swords.

"I had to ask." Kasey grins, his eyes full of laughter.

"You've asked, I've said no. Now, can we get back to the business at hand?"

"Yes, ma'am." He nods, looking not at all serious.

"We'll need to come in and set up some equipment once the papers are signed. Then we'll need to talk to some of the people on the construction crews who ran scared."

"Why?"

"Why what?"

"Why do you need to do all that? Can't you just walk through, and...I don't know…tell them to leave?"

"What happens when you buy a house to flip?"

"We flip it."

"No, what do you do before any construction starts?"

"We bring in the trades, get estimates, have the engineers go over everything."

"Why do you do this?"

"Because we need to know what we're dealing with so we can come up with a construction budget that won't bankrupt me."

"Exactly. These are things you need to know about the house. Same difference with what we do. We need to understand what we're dealing with so we can more effectively take care of the problem at hand."

Kasey nodded. "I never thought of it like that."

"Most people don't think of it at all unless they have need of our services." I pull my phone out of my back pocket and shoot off a text to Dan's dad, who happens to be the attorney for The Hathaway Foundation. I'm glad he decided to move down here with Dan after his wife's murder trial last month. After she tried to kill Dan in the courtroom, neither he nor his other son, Cameron, wanted anything to do with her. She made her bed, and now she is going to lie in it. I am so glad to finally be rid of that woman.

"I texted our attorney, and he'll get the paperwork to you. I just need your email address."

Kasey plucks the phone out of my hands and programs his number into it. "There you go. You've got my number too, in case you need me. Or get bored and just want to talk to me."

I roll my eyes. Today has been such a weird day. Guys normally don't hit on me. At least not anymore. I used to work to make sure I was the center of attention back in my foster care days. Since I met Dan, I don't do that anymore because I only need to be the center of one person's attention. Which I am.

"Cass will be your point person on this. Not me. If you have questions or concerns, he'll do his best to address them."

"I will?"

"You will." I stare him down, willing him to understand Kasey is not a complication I need right now. I don't have the time or the patience to deal with a crush.

"I will."

"Good, now that that's all settled, let's get out of here. I have somewhere to be."

I wait while Cass steers Kasey out of the church before I call for Kane again. He appears instantly. He must have been waiting for Kasey to leave too.

"So, did you find anything?"

"There's something here, something that tastes bad." To anyone else, that probably wouldn't have made sense, but since I can taste emotions and scents much like a cat or a dog, I understand.

"The Loa are here, and they taste…"

"No, it's not the Loa," Kane cuts me off. "Whatever this is, it's got the ghosts scared. I can feel them, but they won't come to me. No, it's more like they refuse to come to me."

"Maybe they're not ready to move on

yet?"

"Maybe, but I can't tell unless they talk to me."

"What do you think is here, then?"

"I don't know, Emma, but whatever it is, be careful. I have to get back to what I was doing. A secret project, if you will. Call me if you need me."

And he's gone. He's getting bad about forgetting to say goodbye. Silas does the same thing, and it annoys me. People should say goodbye.

Looking around one last time, I try to understand why this place is so important to me, but I can't. I feel it in my bones, even if there is no real explanation for it.

Whatever the reason, I will figure out what is going on here.

"So, we're charging for our services now?"

I glance over at Cass, who appears to have waited for me outside the church. His cousins and his car are gone. I'm not surprised. I figured he'd want to talk to me since I sprang the whole fee on him and took over his hunt.

"If they can afford it, sure. The foundation has to be able to pay the hunters, buy the equipment, and cover expenses. Can't do that on empty promises."

"We're gonna get paid?" Surprise flickers across his face.

"Well, duh. Why else would I be

charging him five grand? You, Robert, and Caryle need to be paid. Papa covered the cost of the initial equipment purchases, but we'll need more, and those things are expensive."

"Emma, most hunters doan like de idea of a Crane building a business around hunting."

"I know."

"Do you really, though?"

I nod, keeping my eyes on the road. "Cass, I get it. The Cranes have done some very bad things, but that's not me. I want to help people. I want hunters to have the resources they deserve, to be able to call for backup when needed, and not have to worry about money. What hunters do, it's something that legends will speak of, but I want them safe while they do it. They'll eventually come around."

"I'm no' so sure, *chèr*."

"I am. You up for some lunch?"

"I'm always hungry. You know dis, Emma."

I laugh. I do know. He eats more than I do, and that's saying something. I drive into downtown New Orleans and park at a burger joint a few blocks down from the police department. I promised Dan I'd meet him for lunch. I'm a little early, even with the last-minute ghost hunt. Cass and I go in, and I let the waitress know we'll be expecting one more when she seats us. I shoot a text to Dan to let him know I'm here.

"Dey have good burgers here." Cass picks up the menu and starts scouring it. "You been here before?"

"No. Dan passed by it last week, and since he knows how much I love my bacon cheeseburgers, he suggested we try it out."

"Rob and I eat here when we come into de city." Cass's attention is snagged by two giggling girls a few tables up. He grins lazily at them. Cass is charming on his off days and downright lethal to women on his good days. If not for Dan, I might have been charmed by him too. Well, when I'm not irritated with him. The boy has a habit of irritating me. He's like the little brother I never wished I had. Granted, he's the same age as I am, but still. He feels like a little brother.

"Can I ask you a question?"

"Sure, *chèr*."

"Why do you hide your accent around new people?"

His focus swings back to me and away from the girls. "Wha' you mean?"

"I've noticed it for a while now. When I first met you, you had a bit of an accent, but the longer I knew you, the more it came out. You're straight up Cajun now, but like with Kasey, your accent all but disappeared."

"Dey be a good reason for dat." He leans back and studies the people around him. "For us who grew up on de bayou, it's like we are less den what de normal people are. We're seen as superstitious, illiterate rednecks who'd sooner kill you den look at you."

"But you're not."

He smiles sadly. "I know dat and you know dat, but most doan. People need to be takin' me seriously so I can help dem, an' so I lose de accent. I doan want to be seen as a redneck Cajun."

"You sound like you're speaking from

experience."

"I am, *chèr*. I been on de receiving end of countless slurs and barbs. It wears on a person after a while, so I decided de only people who would know I'm Cajun are de people I trust, de people I call family."

I laugh softly, and he arches a brow.

"You t'ink dis be funny?"

"No. It's just...did you think you'd ever hear yourself admit you'd trust a Crane or consider one family?"

He snorts, a habit he's picked up from me. "Bite your tongue, woman."

I know the minute he steps into the restaurant. It's like an invisible string being pulled, turning my entire being toward him. His soul is connected to mine, but even if it wasn't, I'd still feel him.

Dan Richards, the newest police detective for the New Orleans Police Department and the love of my life. His gaze sweeps the room, coming to stop on me. A blush rises and heats my cheeks. Just one look. That's all it takes from those warm gooey brown eyes of his, and I'm a pile of mush.

Never would I have thought I'd meet someone who can do this to me. Not the girl who only thought about herself, who pushed everyone away so they couldn't hurt her. The old me tried so hard to push Dan away, to make him leave, but he never did. In it for the long haul. Those were always his words to me. Time and time again, he's proven them true. He really is in it for the long haul.

But I'm still me, and I'm afraid one day I will do something to ruin what we have. But until then, I'm going to enjoy what time we have together. I'm going to love him with everything I have.

He doesn't wait for the hostess and makes his way to our table. He's tall, standing a head taller than most people in the room. Since taking on the Sword, everything about him has changed. He's gotten stronger, both physically and mentally. He grew a good six inches, and his muscles became more defined because he started working out. The Sword drove him to be the best, and his efforts at being fit show.

Me, I'd rather face a beating than an

hour at the gym. Thank God I have a high metabolism, or I'd be big as a house, the way I eat.

"Hey, baby." He leans down and kisses me before taking his seat. "Cass. Didn't know you were joining us."

"She's my ride."

"Good to see you, man." Dan nods and rolls his shoulders. He looks tired. "What've you and my girl gotten yourselves into?"

"De-ghosting an old church. Cass didn't like the fact I charged the guy, even though he could afford it."

Dan looks up from the menu, surprised. "You charged him?"

Why is this such a hard thing for people to understand? "Equipment and salaries don't pay for themselves."

"Still..."

"Dan, you were there when we had the meeting about how to pay for The Hathaway Foundation. This is the only idea of Eric's I agreed with. We have to be profitable to help those who can't afford to help themselves."

"Your father donated five million

dollars to the foundation."

Cass's eyes widen. "Say wha'?"

"That money is to purchase a property, build it out to what we need, pay for the initial equipment and funding so we can pay the hunters who call the foundation home. Five million sounds like a lot, but it's not. Not when you start adding up expenses. Just ask your brother. He'll confirm it."

Thankfully, Dan's brother agreed to be our chief financial officer. Cameron is an accountant, but he holds a master's degree in finance. He and his family will be moving down here when school is out in May. Cam didn't want to pull his son out of school in the middle of the year. I can understand that. I used to hate having to move schools so often.

The waitress interrupts us, bringing my and Cass's Cokes and taking our orders. She promises to bring Dan his iced tea right away.

"Have you found a building yet?" Dan asks.

"No. I've been looking, but nothing seems right. We need to be able to build underground, and there's just nothing available that meets those needs."

"Underground?" Cass takes a long pull from his straw.

"Bunkers. The place is going to be a fortress against the supernatural."

"How you likin' N'awlins?" Cass turns his attention to Dan, his subtle way of changing the subject, and I'm glad. I don't want to fight with either of them.

Dan smiles wryly. "It's warm."

"Just wait until summer. You be wishing for dose Carolina summers."

"It can reach over a hundred on any given day during a Carolina summer."

Cass grins wider. "But do you have de same humidity as we get here in de bayou?"

"He's right, Dan. I think Mary lost ten pounds over the summer just from the humidity."

Dan shrugs. "I'm not concerned. I'm cold, for the most part, so I doubt the heat will bother me."

Another truth. Since he came back from the ghost plane, he's colder than he used to be, and I think some of that is because his soul is tied mine. My soul is made up of ghost energy, and I'm always freezing. I hate that for him.

"They figure out where to put you yet?" I smile at the waitress when she sets Dan's drink down. Picking up my own, I take a sip.

"Narcotics."

"What?" I spew the precious Coke right back out. "That's too dangerous!"

"Most new detectives in any state start out in narcotics. We have to pay our dues."

"Will you be going undercover?"

"Possibly." He looks about as nervous as I feel right now. I want to demand he quit, but even as the words try to trip off my tongue, I fight them back. Dan loves his job. He won't quit, and I have no right to ask him to do it.

"Doan worry so much, *chèr*. Dan can take care of himself. I've seen him in action."

"It's one thing to take down a Rougarou and quite another to face the end of a gun. He can't fight a gun with a sword. He might not even see the gun coming."

My hands start to shake as memories of him lying in my arms, bleeding out from a gunshot wound, surface. That moment haunts me. I almost lost him, and the thought of him facing down dealers and addicts who will all be armed with a gun is a little more than I can take.

He pulls my chair to him and wraps an arm around me. It helps, but it doesn't make the memory go away. It only strengthens it.

"Don't go there, Mattie."

"I can't help it," I whisper, tears burning behind my eyelids. "Do you know what that did to me? What it still does to me? I can't lose you, Dan."

"You're not going to lose me." He kisses my temple. "I swear you're not."

"You can't promise me that. Not with your job."

"And you can't promise me one day you won't walk into some hunt and come up against something you can't handle either. We both have dangerous jobs, but neither of us would change that."

He's right. I know it, and he knows it,

but it doesn't help.

"Dis be an easy fix." Cass grins like the Cheshire cat.

"What do you mean?"

"Wha' time you get off work?"

"Six tonight. Why?"

"We get you de same protection we have. You too, Emma."

"Protection?"

"Dey be a tattoo shop who deals in protection tats. Dey can get you one to make sure a gunshot woan kill you. It can't stop de bullet, but it can slow down de damage so you don't die."

"Maybe we should have Silas do it."

Dan's face darkens. He does not like Silas, not that I can blame him. He almost died once because of my demonic grandfather.

"No."

"Dan..."

He shakes his head. "No. That demon isn't touching me."

He's still a little mad that Silas knocked him out to give him the same protection against fallen angels that I have on my back. The same one that now graces Mary, Eric, and even Mary's mom. I was afraid they'd go after her because she's important to me. The woman agreed without hesitation. I'm still trying to figure out how to protect Nancy. Zeke knows about the Fallen Angels plotting revenge, and he's doing everything he can to keep her safe, but he knows as well as I do that we need to tell her about us. But I understand why he hasn't. He doesn't want to lose her any more than I do.

"You trust these people?" I ask Cass.

"*Oui, chèr*, I do. Dey be de ones who do all de ink for most hunters in de area."

"And you're sure this tattoo will protect him?"

Cass nods. "I been shot on more den one occasion. De protection tat kept me alive."

He laughs at my expression. I can believe a lot, but the thought of a ghost shooting him is more than I can buy.

"Ah, *chèr*, I forget you doan know dat much about our world. It's more den just ghosts and Rougarous. Dey be a whole world dat uses modern-day weapons as well as supernatural abilities. You come up against a vamp or a were, dey be just as likely to be packing some heat as dey are to try to drain you or shift and kill you. Guns be easier den trying to explain o'der t'ings."

Now it's Dan's turn to look worried. I don't think he realized I could face the same dangers he does every day. Neither did I, for that matter. I hate guns. *Hate them.*

"Can you set up an appointment for him tonight?"

"Hey, now, don't I get a say in this?" Dan's fingers rub slow circles into my arm, doing his best to calm me down.

"No. If you won't let Silas do it, then you're going to trust Cass's people. I won't let you go out there unprotected if I can help it. So just shut up and say, 'thank you, Cass.'"

"How am I supposed to thank him if I shut up?" Dan grins, his eyes twinkling.

I shake my head, grateful for the food arriving. The waitress frowns at my having moved my chair, or rather Dan moving it, but she doesn't say anything.

Smart lady. I'm not in the mood and would have told her off. Between flashes of that awful day in the courtroom and worrying about Dan being assigned to narcotics, my good mood went out the window.

At least I have a way of keeping him somewhat safe now. It's a good thing Cass was here, or I would never have known about the protection tat for gunshots.

And Dan wonders why I have so much faith. It's because of things like this, when I'm drowning in fear and worry, when hope shines through. It's why I know I'm not alone, why I never lose my faith.

To me, the child of a goddess, I still have faith in my religion. I believe in God and all that He does because I see the small things every day.

It's what kept me from completely giving up in foster care. I knew I wasn't alone.

And that faith brought me my family. It brought me Dan. It brought me Eli and then gave me the strength to go on when

Eli died. It brought me Mary, Eric, and Cass. Dan may never understand why I believe, but that doesn't matter. All that matters is that I do, and I'm thankful for all the blessings that came this ex-foster girl's way.

Smiling, I dig into my very delicious bacon cheeseburger, some of my fear and panic receding as I feel the comfort of my faith keep me strong yet again.

"Papa?"

His office is empty when I manage to drag myself to his house. I know he's home. I texted him before coming over. I dropped Cass off and drove straight here. I need a favor, one I think Zeke can help me with. Hopefully.

"He's in the kitchen, Miss Emma."

Jameson, my father's butler, is standing in the doorway, an amused smile playing with his lips at having startled me.

"No sneaking, Jameson. We've had this conversation before."

"I wasn't sneaking, Miss Emma. I heard you shouting."

I'm not sure Jameson is much older than my father. He still has a full head of hair with only a few grays starting to show at his temples. I wonder how long he's actually worked for Papa.

"Is Mrs. Banks cooking?"

Even though I just ate lunch, if my father's housekeeper and cook is preparing a meal, I will make room. She is the absolute best cook in the world. I tell her all the time she needs to open her own restaurant. She only smiles and tells me she's happy where she is.

"I believe she's making your father a late lunch, yes."

I waste no more time and breeze past Jameson and head directly to the kitchen where I find my father sitting at the informal table. He prefers to eat in here as opposed to the dining room. Lila hates that, having raised him with proper manners and all that rot, but he defies her when she's not around. I secretly think he's terrified of his mother.

"Hi, Papa." I bend to kiss him on the cheek before taking a seat beside him. He doesn't look like me. I look like my mother, Georgina Dubois. Zeke reminds me of that actor who plays Ichabod Crane on Fox's *Sleepy Hollow*. He looks like him, right down to the long hair.

"*Ma petite.*" Zeke puts his paper down. "Are you hungry?"

"Well, I did just have lunch with Dan and Cass."

Mrs. Banks snorts, and I grin at her. She's standing by the stove, heaping out two large bowls of her blackened chicken alfredo. She knows me too well.

"And?" Zeke tries to fight his own grin.

"I could eat."

"Of course, you can." Mrs. Banks puts the bowl down in front of me, sprinkling fresh parmesan cheese over it. Her dark brown hair is pulled back into a ponytail, making her look younger than she actually is. I think she's in her mid-forties, but I'm not sure. She looks about thirty-five, but again, who knows? One thing I've noticed is that lots of people in New Orleans look a lot younger than they are. I often wonder if they all have really good genes or if more people than admit partake of magic to keep them looking so spry. It's a question I intend to get an answer to one day, but not today. Chicken alfredo is calling my name.

I lean down and take a deep breath, letting the smell take me to food heaven. I love this stuff. "Mrs. B, you are gonna have to teach me to make this so I can surprise Dan. He thinks I burn water."

"You do."

I laugh at her droll comment. It's true. I did burn water, and I set a TV dinner on fire in the microwave once when I was living with Mary and her mom. They both agreed it would be best for me not to try to start dinner again. I do, however, make a mean salad.

"Will you teach me, though?"

"You want to learn to cook?" Mrs. Banks looks surprised.

I nod. "I need to be able to feed Dan without setting anything on fire or giving him food poisoning."

"Food poisoning?" Zeke quirks a brow in question.

"We won't talk about that." I tried to make a simple recipe once and ended up giving us both food poisoning. Dan and I do not mention said incident.

Zeke chuckles and digs into his food. His appetite is as big as mine.

"If you really want to learn, honey, I will be more than happy to teach you." Mrs. Bank takes a seat at the table, bringing her own bowl of food, something else Lila would have a conniption fit over. One does not eat with the staff.

"I do." I spear a piece of chicken and all but drool. If my metabolism ever slows down, I'm sunk. I love food too much.

"What brings you by, *ma petite*? Don't you have class?"

"Nah. I have my last final in the morning, and then you're stuck with me, Mary, and Eric until the new semester begins."

Zeke makes a noncommittal noise, but he secretly loves the fact that the three of us will be staying with him. He missed out on raising me, so every minute he spends with me now is that much more precious to him. And to me. Growing up with no one, I appreciate my father and all he does for me, but more than anything, I love being loved. I never really understood love until Dan Richards. If not for him, the relationship between me and Zeke would be a completely different one.

"But as to why I'm here, I need a favor."

Now, that gets his attention. I never ask my dad for anything.

"What can you tell me about The Red Church?"

Both he and Mrs. Banks stop eating and stare at me, Zeke's fork midway to his mouth.

"Why do you want to know about that?" Mrs. Banks asks.

"Because I'm helping Cass with it. He's pissed at me because I'm charging the guy who owns it for our services, but he can afford it."

"You need to stay away from there." Mrs. Bank folds her napkin and places it on the table, staring me right in the eyes. "It's a bad place, sweetheart, one that would smell your innocence and eat you alive."

Zeke shakes his head. "It's not that bad. I'm even considering investing in the property."

"Kasey told me. That's why I figured you'd know the history of the place and might be able to pull a few strings to get me information that's not readily available."

"What kind of information?"

"Simon said the Vatican had all the journals of the priests and nuns who died there. I was hoping you might be able to find someone to tell me about those journals and what they contain. I know they'll never let me see them, but I need to know what happened there. What *really* happened. Not what the church told people happened."

Zeke's expression turns calculating. It's a look I know well since it's one I wear quite often. He's up to something.

"I'll make you a deal."

See? I knew he was up to something.

"If you go to Christmas Eve mass with me, I'll see if I can find someone with the information you want."

"I'm not Catholic, Papa."

He shrugs. "You believe in God. That's all that counts."

"If you want me to come with you, you have to do better than 'see' if you can find someone. You *will* find someone."

Zeke laughs. "You've been around Silas too much."

It's my turn to shrug. Silas does deals all day long. I've learned enough to know when I'm getting a bad one.

"Ezekiel, you cannot send her in there." Mrs. Banks has been quiet since that first statement, but we both turn to her, surprised. She's not someone who tends to be superstitious, and being around the Cranes, she understands more about the supernatural world than I do.

"Mrs. B, I was already there. It doesn't feel any weirder than any other haunted house."

"You don't know what's there, what happened…why it happened."

"But you do?" Zeke asks, his voice mild.

"You know I do. I already told you not to invest in that cursed place. I thought you had more common sense than this, Ezekiel Crane." She gets up and walks out of the room, leaving her food behind.

"What was that all about?"

"There's more to her than you know, *ma petite*. Secrets that aren't mine to tell."

She has secrets? I file that away for later discovery.

"Is she right, though? I honestly didn't feel anything overly evil there."

"I don't know, Emma. I inspected the property as well and only felt a few frightened souls. I will say this. Mrs. Banks knows more about the evil in New Orleans than most. If she says there's something there, we'd do well to head her advice."

"I still have to help Kasey, Papa. I promised."

"I know." He nods and picks up his fork. "You have this insane need to help people. I'm still unsure where you got that."

"From you, of course." Papa does so much to help people that no one knows about, like food and medicine shipments to underdeveloped countries, to villages who would die without the goods he sends them.

He winks at me. "Don't be saying that out loud. I have a reputation to protect. It's that same reputation that will get us the donations we need to continue that good work. Can't have our guests this weekend thinking I'm soft."

I groan at the reminder of this weekend's charity ball. I'd all but forgotten about it and my fight with Lila. I should probably tell him about it before Lila does.

"Lila and I had a fight."

Zeke frowns. "What about?"

"Nancy."

"What about Nancy?"

"She alluded to the fact that she's not good enough to be dating you."

"She what?" The soft tone my father uses is deceptive, but I know him well enough to know his anger has spiked a ten on the Richter scale.

"She made a remark about Nancy not coming from the same class of wealth as you guys, and I lost it on her. I shouldn't have spoken to her like that, but I couldn't help it, and I won't apologize for it either. Nancy is the closest thing I have to a mother, and I won't let anyone talk about her or put her down."

"*Non, ma petite*, you will not apologize to my mother. She had no right to say that. I love Nancy, and Mama will accept that or not, but I will not allow her to treat Nancy with anything but respect."

"She wouldn't treat her any other way while Nancy is present, Papa. It's what she says behind closed doors that set my blood boiling. And it's not just Nancy. It's me too. Sometimes I think she thinks the same about me. She loves me, I know she does, but I don't think like her. I don't act like her. I hate shopping and parties, and I feel like I let her down all the time. That might have been part of why I got so mad. What she said about Nancy, it hit home with me, and I felt so dejected in that one second."

"Sweetheart." Zeke gets up and pulls me out of my chair and into a hug so tight, it's hard to breathe. "Your *grandmère* adores you. You are the reason she gets up every day. She fought so hard to help me find you. She never gave up hope. None of us did. We knew we'd find you one day."

"I know she loves me, Papa."

"You could never disappoint her. Don't think like that. You *grandmère*…she's a hard woman to get to know and an even harder woman to understand. But one thing I promise you, she's not disappointed in you. She'll never be disappointed in you."

I'm not so sure about that. Lila is from old money. She has this air, this way about her that speaks to that. I don't think she'd even admit to herself how much of a disappointment I am to her, but I feel it. And I can't help how I feel any more than she can.

"Would she be disappointed if I don't come to the party?"

"You really hate them, don't you?"

I nod against his chest. "I really do."

"You're going to have to get used to them, though, *ma petite*. Those same donors are the ones who will write the big checks to The Hathaway

Foundation."

"Is that why you insisted I come?" I look up at him. "So I could make the connections I need in order to run the foundation?"

"Partly. But I also enjoy having you there. You keep me from getting bored."

"The last party I attended, I accidentally spilled my drink on that lady with the too shiny dress. She blinded me."

Zeke chuckles, remembering the incident. "Like I said, you keep things interesting."

"I can't ditch it, then?"

"*Non, ma petite*, you can't ditch it. I expect you to be there with your Christmas bells on."

"Fine. Now, about that deal. You will find someone to talk to me?"

His eyes twinkle. Never a good sign with Zeke.

"*Oui, ma petite*, I will find someone to talk to you." He lets me go and takes Mrs. Banks's bowl of pasta to the fridge. "Now, let's eat and not worry about the things we can do nothing about."

I'm not foolish enough to think he's forgotten about Lila and Nancy or how I feel, but I follow his lead and drop it. We'll deal with all that later. Right now, we have a perfectly good bowl of alfredo to consume.

I've avoided going to my dorm room all day. I spent the afternoon with Zeke helping him to decorate for Christmas. Nancy was supposed to help him, but she got caught up at the hospital with one of her foster kids, so I pitched in instead. It was a lot of fun. Last year, I hadn't been in a good place, and even though Mary and I had helped to decorate, our hearts hadn't been in it. Neither of us has gotten over our ordeal with Deleriel, the Fallen Angel I destroyed, but we're handling it a lot better this year.

Christmas does that, though. It has a tendency to heal when nothing else can. Even last year, although we hadn't completely gotten into Christmas, we'd both been better afterward.

I know the minute I step foot in my dorm room Mary and Eric will be on me to start filming for the first episode of The Ghost Girl, our YouTube channel. I so do not want to do it, but telling Mary no is like kicking a puppy and laughing. You just can't do it.

Hence why I'm waiting in the parking lot of Dan's apartment building. I texted to let him know I'd meet him here so we could go meet up with Cass's tattoo artist. I'm debating calling Silas to make sure they're legit once we get there. No need to tell Dan beforehand. He'll just argue and get all huffy.

If not for leaving Mary alone, I'd spend the night at Dan's. Neither Mary nor I can be alone at night. We still have horrific nightmares. We might not talk about them, but we're there for each other. Even when I marry Dan, he's accepted the fact Mary will have a room in our home for this very reason. It's why he has a two-bedroom apartment now. If I spend the night, so does Mary.

It's not long before his death trap of a truck pulls in. He spots me as soon as he gets out, and I debate if we should take my car. His truck gives me hives. I'm always expecting it to break down when we're in the middle of nowhere. But people will be less likely to strip his truck down for parts. My car is a Lexus, and I treat it like the precious baby it is. The cost of the car is enough to make my stomach queasy, so I take care of it in return. Zeke didn't even blink at the cost, but I did. I tried to get out of accepting it, but I can't say no to my father any more than I can Mary.

So I drag myself out of the comfort of my car and over to where Dan is just getting out of the death trap. The smile he sends my way is heart melting.

"Hey, baby. I would have picked you up at the dorm." His arms slide around me, and he leans down for a quick kiss that turns into a longer one.

"Somebody missed me," I say when he pulls back.

"Always."

"You ready to go get a tattoo?"

The smile vanishes. "Do we really have to?"

"Unless you want me so paranoid I'm texting you every second of every day, then yes, we have to."

"If I go undercover, you won't be able to reach me until the assignment is done."

He had to go and tell me that, didn't he? I lean my forehead against his chest. He doesn't need to see the panic rising. I've almost lost him more times than I can count, once at the hands of his own mother. I know he loves his job, but it's going to be the death of me.

"Hey." He tips my chin up so I have to look at him. "It's going to be okay. I promise."

"Do you have to take narcotics? Can't you do homicide or something? Where the victims are already dead and don't carry guns?"

"Narcotics was the only thing they offered, Mattie. It's typically where all new detectives start. I already told you this."

"I know, but I don't have to like it. The thought of you getting shot…" I break off, unable to go there again. I've never been more scared in my life than I was when he was shot.

"Don't think about that day. It's behind us."

"But it's not. Every single day, it's right there in front of us. Whenever you go to work, it's all I think about. That's why I was so happy you got promoted to detective. I thought you'd be safer."

"I will be safer."

"Not in narcotics, you won't. I watch *Law and Order* and *Blue Bloods*. I know all about narcotics."

He smiles, and I know he's trying to pacify me. I won't be pacified. Not when it comes to his safety.

"Don't believe everything you see on TV. Real life is very different."

"What about *Cops* or the live police show? They aren't scripted."

He frowns, not having anything to say to that.

"I'm just worried, Dan. And scared. I can't lose you."

It's moot, though. If he dies, I die. Our souls are tied together, but Silas believes

I won't die if Dan does. He thinks whatever Rhea did to me will protect me from Dan's death. The thing is, though, if he dies and I don't, I won't make it. Eli's death was hard, but Dan? I know wouldn't survive it. It's a simple truth I feel in my bones.

"You're not going to lose me. It's why I agreed to get inked up for you."

He hates having all those protection tattoos, but he does it without question. For me. So I know he's got that little bit of extra protection.

"We'd better get going, or we'll be late." I pull away from him and go around to get into the truck. Time for a subject change. "When are you retiring this thing to the museum?"

He glares and pats the dashboard. "She doesn't mean it, girl. You're a good truck."

I roll my eyes. I love my car too, but I don't talk to it. Dan seems to think his truck can hear him. Ridiculous, but he's not the only one. I'd heard Eric doing the same thing to his car. Guys and their vehicles.

He starts the truck and backs up. "Eric called me. He wanted to know where you are."

"What did you tell him?" I can't keep the panic out of my voice. I do not want to do that stupid YouTube show.

"That you were helping me this evening with something. I know you've been avoiding your sister and Eric for a couple days now."

"I hate doing it, but I hate the thought of doing a YouTube show even more. It gives me hives."

"Is it because they want you to showcase your abilities, or is it the show in general?"

I reach over and turn the heat on full blast. "A little of both, I think. I came here to escape my past, not embrace it. I don't want anyone to see me and say 'look, there's the weird girl from YouTube who says she can see ghosts.'"

"But you can see ghosts, and I thought you loved helping them move on."

"I do, but that doesn't mean I want millions of people knowing about it."

"Babe, no one will really think you can

see ghosts." I give him a look, and he hurries to continue. "Well, there will be a few who do, but for the most part, they'll all think you're putting on a show. And in the process, you might actually find a few people who really need your help."

"It'll be just one more reason for Lila to be disappointed in me."

Dan glances my way and then back to the road. "What are you talking about?"

I tell him about our fight and how I think she's disappointed in me even if she'll never admit it. I'm not as close to my grandparents as I am to Zeke, and maybe that's why I can't shake these feelings.

"Sweetheart, your grandparents love you, and one thing I've learned about the Cranes is they don't care what anyone thinks. You're one of them. No, you didn't grow up going to fancy schools, and you hate the idea of having money, but you are a Crane, and to a Crane, that's all that matters. Lila has Mary to go shopping with her. Mary helps her plan her parties. All she wants from you is you."

"I'm surprised they took to Mary and Eric like they did. Lila insists they call her *grandmère*."

And I don't mind that one bit. Eric needs all the family he can get. And Mary? She's a shopping freak. I think all the retail therapy helped her more than actual therapy did sometimes. Spending time with Lila is good for her.

"So, you see, Lila doesn't need any of that from you. She only needs you to be you."

"Maybe."

Dan lets it drop, and the silence that ensues is comfortable. Neither of us feels the need to fill up the silence with useless chatter. Dan drives us to the very outskirts of New Orleans. The tattoo shop he pulls up in front of has a few bikers hanging around and a few people who may or may not be drug dealers. It's not a safe place.

Thankfully, Cass is already waiting for us and gets out of his car as soon as he spots us. Dan has on his patented Officer Dan look, the one I try to perfect and fail miserably. He looks bored, but he's taking in everything, from the bikers to the druggies to how well-lit the exterior of the building is. He's a cop through and through. Which is why I can never ask him to give up doing what he loves. He'd be miserable.

"What's up, Spider?" Cass nods to one of the bikers leaning against the building, smoking.

The big biker turns to look his way. "Not much. Just waitin' on the new guy to get his tats done. You here to get some new ink?"

"No, my friends are. Spider, dis be Emma Crane and her boyfriend, Dan Richards. Emma's a hunter."

"Crane?" Hazel eyes very much like my own study me.

"She be Ezekiel Crane's daughter."

Spider nods. "Your father has done us a few solids over the years. You're safe here, *chèr*."

Zeke has had dealings with biker gangs? One more thing to add to the growing lists of questions for my papa. The man gets around.

"Spider is the president of the Devil's

Sins motorcycle club. His MC owns this shop." Cass points to the sign. Devil's Ink. "You should see some of dis girl's artwork, Spider. She be de one who drew the dragon on my back."

That earns me a more speculative stare. "You good with drawing?"

I nod, and Dan moves in closer, not trusting these guys any more than I do.

"We best be gettin' inside." Cass holds the door open, and Dan's hand on my back pushes me toward the open door. For once, I'm not gonna argue with him. This place gives me the heebie jeebies.

The inside is cleaner than the outside. There's no trash, and the floors look freshly mopped. A girl sits chewing bubble gum and looking through a magazine at the front desk. Her blonde hair is pulled up into a high ponytail, showcasing the tattoos climbing her neck and bleeding into her hairline. They're very precise and well done. It gives me hope the artist here won't screw up.

"Cass." She throws her magazine down and comes around the counter to hug him. He blushes slightly, and I quirk a brow. He looks everywhere but at me. Dan chuckles, sensing the boy has a crush on this girl too.

"Melinda." Cass hugs her back then turns her attention toward us. "Let me introduce you to Emma Crane and her boyfriend, Dan Richards."

Sea green eyes dance with mirth when she turns them on us. She seems like a happy girl. If she didn't have all the tattoos, I wouldn't peg her for someone working in a tattoo shop.

"Dey be here to get a protection tat."

"Which one?"

"De gun one."

"Ah, that's a popular one." She nods and goes back behind the counter, collecting two clipboards with paperwork attached. "You'll need to fill these out. Just some basic questions and information."

We take the forms and sit down. The chairs are generic and hard, not meant to encourage people to hang out. It only takes us a minute to fill everything out. As Melinda said, it's all basic information.

"So, what do you all need a gun protection tat for?"

Cass shakes his head at her, but Dan smiles. "I'm a cop. My girlfriend has her heart set on getting me all the protection she can."

"You brought a cop here?" Melinda's gaze sharpens, and her expression closes off.

"I trust dem, *chèr*. Dey have had my back on more den one occasion."

"Spider's not gonna be happy."

"Spider met dem outside."

"Did you tell him he's a cop?"

"No, but dat shouldn't matter. His money be just as good as anyone else's."

"If this is a problem, we can leave." Dan frowns at them.

Cass and I both say "no" together.

"You won't let Silas do the tat, so this is your only other option." I turn in my seat to face him. "It's your choice. Silas or here."

"He's not touching me ever again."

"Then you're gonna suck it up and deal with people who aren't fond of cops."

"If I remember right, you aren't too

fond of cops yourself." He grins at me.

"You're the exception."

Just then a very bulky guy emerges from the hallway, a bandage peeking out from beneath the shirt sleeve of his right shoulder. He's covered in tats, even his face. He should scare me, but instead, I find myself fascinated by the artwork his body has become. The designs are intricate and at first, appear random, but that's not the case. It's an evolving piece, each image feeding into the others.

He glares in our direction. "Got a problem?"

"No. I just think your tats are pretty awesome."

A slow smile curves his lips. "You like tattoos, sugar?"

"Not particularly, but I do find the artwork fascinating."

"Want to go find it fascinating somewhere a little more private?"

I don't have time to say a word before Dan is up and standing in front of me. He grows taller, wider in that second. The sword blazes on his back, blinding me. Even Cass seems to sense the danger because he hurries over to Dan.

"She's mine." The words come out harshly, and his usual warm eyes have gone cold. Gone is Officer Dan, and in his place is a Warrior of the Sword.

Biker dude takes a step back, trying to get a read on Dan. He didn't seem like a threat at first, but this version of Officer Dan is downright scary.

"Emma's off limits." Cass steps up beside Dan. "Got it?"

Biker dude's eyes swivel from between the two of them, and then he shrugs, skirting around them and heading to the front to pay Melinda.

"What is it with you today, *chèr*?" Cass shakes his head at me.

"What do you mean?" Dan asks, turning to make sure biker dude leaves.

Cass seems to realize what he said, and I'm trying to warn him with my eyes.

"No'tin."

Dan's about to argue the point when another guy comes out of the back. He's covered in tats, but he's skinnier than the bikers outside. Doesn't make him feel less dangerous, though. The vibe he gives off is more violent than the other bikers. I don't know if I want him touching me or Dan.

"Cass." He nods toward us. "These your friends?"

"*Oui*, dis be Emma and Dan."

Eyes as black as a demon's give us the once-over. "You never told me why they would need a gun protection tat."

"Dan's a cop," Cass says and holds up a hand before the guy can say anything. "He's not like that. You can trust him."

"And her?"

"She's Emma Crane."

The guy's nostrils flare. "Crane?"

"She be his daughter, and Dan's her boyfriend."

"I'm Needle." The guy shoves a hand through his messy blond hair. "Come on back."

We follow him into one of the tattoo rooms. There's a chair and a table in the room. The table would be for body parts not reachable in the chair. It brings back memories of all the times Silas has inked me. A tray with the tattoo needle and some ink bottles is between them. One of those rolly stools you see in doctors' offices is at the bottom of the table.

The floors are clean, the walls covered in artwork. Most of the designs are dark, but then I do dark very well. I find myself drawn to them and wander over to get a little more in-depth look at the dragon riding the back of a three-headed dog. Strange. I would have thought it would be vice versa, but the sketch is so well done, it doesn't appear odd at all.

"These are beautiful."

"Thank you." Needle is right behind me, and I jump at his nearness. "Sorry, didn't mean to scare you."

"You didn't. It's been a long day full of strange things."

"No stranger than having Ezekiel Crane's daughter in my shop."

"I got you beat. I spent the afternoon at The Red Church."

The man physically shrinks away from me. Just another clue that there is more to whatever haunts that place than I felt. It had hidden well from me.

"You shouldn't be there. That place…it's bad juju."

"It won't be when I'm done with it." With a sigh, I tear myself away from the artwork. "Now, what design do you typically do for this gun protection tattoo?"

"A gun." A nervous smile plays with his lips. My mentioning the Red Church seems to have unnerved him a bit. His reaction isn't as severe as Mrs. Banks, but it's telling.

"No guns. I hate guns."

"We can find something else for you. The magic's in the ink, anyway."

"No guns for Dan either."

Needle looks to Dan for confirmation. "I want a sword instead."

"A sword."

I reach into my bag and pull out my sketchbook. "This sword."

Needle takes the book from me when I've found the correct page. "Did you do this?"

"Sure did."

He looks through the book, a speculative look coming into his eyes. "You want a job?"

"What?" I blink at him, unsure I heard

him right.

"A job, *chèr*. My other tattoo artist, Crawl, wound up in jail and I ain't found anyone who did work even half as decent as he did. These are beautiful. If you can ink skin as well as you do paper, you have a job if you want it."

I half expect Dan to shout no, but he knows I have common sense.

"Thanks for the offer, but I'm good."

"We're not as bad as you think. Those men out there will protect you with their life."

"Be that as it may, I'm good."

He shrugs. "You figure out what you want while I ink him."

Dan doesn't look too happy, but he sits in the chair.

"Where do you want it?"

"The inside of his arm." I walk over and help Dan out of his shirt. "Start the pommel of the sword handle here at the top of his shoulder and ink it all the way down the inside of his arm, the sword's tip ending in the palm of his hand."

"Those are some serious tats." Needle is inspecting the full body tattoo that goes from the back of Dan's neck all the way down to his toes. It's the one that keeps him hidden from Fallen Angels. Several others are woven into the design to protect him from a whole host of baddies.

We both ignore Needle's obvious appreciation of the tattoo.

"Mattie, I can't have a tattoo like that. It's against regulations."

"You have invisible ink?"

"I don't, but I can get it." He cocks his head. "I thought your name was Emma?"

"It is, but Mattie's my name too. When do you think you'll have to start in narcotics?"

"Next week."

"Can you get it by the weekend?"

Needle nods.

"We'll be back Saturday, then." I toss Dan his shirt and take my sketchbook back from Needle. "Can you book us an appointment on Saturday?"

"Stop out and see Randi. She'll get you in."

"Thanks." I take Dan's hand and pull him along with me back the front desk. We make our appointments, say our goodbyes to Cass, and then head back outside. No one has touched his truck, thankfully. Not that I thought they would. The thing really does belong in an automobile museum.

"The dorm or my place?"

"Let's grab a pizza and head to the dorm. I've hidden from my family long enough, but if we bring food, they might forgive me."

"We're not done talking about that comment Cass made."

And here I hoped he'd forgotten about that little remark.

"Can we talk about it tomorrow? I think I've had enough of a crappy day."

"Sure, baby, but we are gonna talk about it."

Dan starts the truck and pulls out while I turn on the heat. One bullet dodged for today, at least.

The heavenly scent of rich coffee assaults my nose. Hazelnut syrup follows. It's enough to make me crack an eye with the sunlight pouring through the windows. Mary's humming as she makes two mugs of the delicious brew.

"I know you're awake," my sister says. "Might as well get up or I'll drink both of these."

"You wouldn't dare."

She flashes me an evil grin over her shoulder. She would.

I sit up and rub my eyes. "What time is it?"

"It's a little after seven. We both have a final at eight."

"Last one for me." Thank God for small miracles.

"I have one more this afternoon and I'm done." She pushes her heavy blonde hair out of her face and then picks up both cups, coming over to sit on my bed and handing me one. "You okay?"

"Yeah, why?"

"You were screaming in your sleep last night."

"I was? I don't remember dreaming anything."

"You were muttering about nuns."

Crap. I guess maybe my psyche took more of a beating than I knew. "It had to be the church Cass took me to."

"You were screaming because you visited a church?"

"No." I set my mug of coffee on the bedside table and lean down to drag my laptop out from under the bed. The last page I was looking at is still blinking when I open it. It's a page from the historical society about The Red Church. "Here, read through it while I drink my coffee, or I'll be useless."

"Oh my God, why would you want me

to read this?"

I blow on the coffee before taking a sip. The burst of hazelnut hits my tongue, and I groan out loud. Mary makes a mean pot of coffee.

"It's the first official case of The Hathaway Foundation."

"Really? How did Cass take it? I know he's against charging people for his hunting services."

"He wasn't happy with it, but I hope once he sees the equipment, he'll understand we need to make money to sustain everything."

"He'll come around. When are you going back to set up?"

"I need to do some research first, then I'll probably go back later this afternoon or tomorrow."

"Maybe you should wait until in the morning." Her eyes are fixed on the screen. "This place is a murder house, Em."

"Mrs. Banks told me to stay away from there. She had the strangest reaction when I told her. I mean Zeke's thinking about investing in the place, but Mrs. B flipped out."

"Seriously?"

I nod, still disturbed by her reaction. "She's never done that before, and you know working for Zeke, she has to have seen some pretty freaky stuff. She knows all about his dealings in the supernatural."

"Huh. Now I know I don't want you anywhere near that place close to nightfall. Promise me you won't go there by yourself."

"I promise." I have no intention of setting foot in that place by myself. Not after everyone's weird reactions. "You packed up yet?"

"No." She takes a sip of her own coffee. "I keep putting it off. I don't know if I want to leave our Christmas wonderland."

Like I said before, it looks like Santa's elves threw up in here, and I love it as much as she does.

"I helped Zeke decorate yesterday, so trust me, it's not boring. Plus, he said we could add any decorations we want to any room in the house. Lila will be disgusted with it when we're done."

"Which reminds me. We need to go shopping for a dress for the party this weekend."

I moan out loud at the thought, and Mary laughs at me. "You know I hate shopping."

"Yes, but that's why you have me. I'll get you in and out in record time."

God bless Mary for her shopping skills. They even rival my old best friend, Meg's. Thinking about her sends a pang through my heart. I miss her sometimes. Doesn't mean I'm not still pissed she violated the best friend code and dated Dan when she knew I didn't know how I felt about him. I forgave her, though. Her death will always haunt me because she was one of the few people who mattered to me.

"Hey, where'd you go?"

"Sorry, just thinking about Meg. She took me shopping for the last big party I attended."

Neither of us mentions the fact it was that same party that Meg and I were both kidnapped from and resulted in Meg's death.

Happy times.

"Tell you what, once our final is over, we'll head over to the pancake place and have breakfast. Eric should be done by then as well."

Please, I don't want to talk about the channel...please....

"We can talk about our first episode of Ghost Girl."

I deflate like a balloon.

"Mary, I don't want to do it. I really, really don't. Why don't you start a fashion channel or something? You love clothes and shopping and..."

"And this is something I think will help people, Em." She refuses to call me Emma, but she caved on Em. It's the sound of the M from the name Mattie, and it can still refer to Emma. Like Dan, I'll always be Mattie to her.

"How? How will it help people?" I put the mug down and get up and start hunting for clothes. "All it'll do is single me out as the weird girl who sees ghosts. I came here to get away from all that."

"But you help ghosts all the time."

"Where I can't be seen doing it."

"No one's going to believe you really see ghosts."

"Then why are you pushing me to do this?"

"Because…" She pauses and frowns at me. "You really don't want to do this, do you?"

"No. I really don't want to do this. Being the Ghost Girl, it brings back memories I'd rather forget. Memories that haunt my dreams. Memories I run from every single minute of every day. Please, don't make me do this, Mary. If you and Eric want to do it, I'll support you and help in any way I can, but I don't want to be your star."

Her blue eyes well with tears. "I'm so sorry, Mattie. I didn't know it was bringing back bad memories. You know I'd never do anything to hurt you."

"I know." I sit back down beside her. "After the whole Rougarou thing, my feelings are hypersensitive. Every single thing I've buried came out, and no matter how hard I try, I can't shove it all back down. I even blew up at Lila yesterday."

"You did?"

I tell her about my verbal vomit and hang my head. I should apologize to my grandmother, but I can't. No, it's more that I won't.

Mary wraps an arm around me. "I'm sorry."

"Me too. I didn't mean to blow up at you a minute ago."

"No, you should have done that months ago. I really didn't know you were this against it. Eric and I'll figure something out. I'm not going to make you do this if you don't want to."

"Thank you."

"Let's get dressed, or we're going to be late for our finals."

For the first time in months, I'm not walking around like an anxiety ball, ready to explode with the barest of touches. Mary allowing me to walk away from her YouTube project was the best Christmas present I could ever ask for.

***

Eric Cameron, AKA Jake Owens,

AKA Mirror Boy.

He's my best friend, my brother, my family. I am here today because of him and everything he sacrificed to keep me safe. I love him.

He's also a pain in my behind.

But I wouldn't trade him for anyone or anything.

Except maybe today. He's shoveling pancakes into his mouth faster than the poor girl can bring them. I'd swear he never gets food, but I know better. He eats with me and Mary on a regular basis.

Hair so black it glints blue surfs the top of his shirt collar. He's let it grow out quite bit, but it doesn't detract from the bluest eyes I've ever seen. Mary's eyes are sky blue, but Eric's are electric. They glint like jewels, and the color is clear and bright and just downright beautiful.

But then so is Eric. Sure, his soul is in my ex-boyfriend's body, who was cute to begin with. But Eric is beautiful through and through. He has a heart bigger than Texas, and he's a flirt. Even with me and Mary. Drives Dan nuts sometimes, but I think Eric does it just to get a rise out of my boyfriend.

"Remind me never to eat in public with him again," Mary says, disgusted. She pushes her own plate of pancakes to the side. "I'm not even hungry anymore."

Eric flashes her a smile full of half-eaten pancakes, and she turns away.

"You sure you don't want those?" I point to her plate.

"Take it."

I waste no time in sliding her pancakes onto my own plate. Eric doesn't gross me out like he does Mary. "You done with finals yet, Eric?"

"Yup. Finished my last one this morning, thank God." He downs half a glass of milk. "You?"

"Me too. Mary has one more this afternoon. You packed up?"

He nods. "My mom is upset I'm not coming back to Charlotte for Christmas, though."

"I thought she might be. Do you want to go home?"

"No." He pops a piece of bacon into his mouth. "It's not really home for me. She cried the last time I was there because I didn't remember something. I'm never going to have Jake's memories, and it hurts them. I hate doing that."

"That makes no sense." Ethan Cooper plops down beside Eric and snatches a piece of bacon.

"Get your own," Eric growls at him, but there's no heat to it. I have a feeling he'd share his last morsel with the guy. For reasons he's not ready to admit to yet.

"What makes no sense?" Mary finishes off her orange juice.

"Who's Jake, and why will you never have his memories?"

We all get quiet, and Ethan stares at us, confused.

"Eric's name is Jacob Eric Owens. He used to be called Jake," I explain. "He got shot and hit his head when he fell. He had no memory of who he was when he woke up. He doesn't remember being Jake, and it was easier for him for us to call him Eric instead. His parents do remember Jake and how he used to be. Eric's not Jake. He'll never be Jake, and it hurts them all."

"Dude, you never told me that." Nathan's brown eyes go a little wide. "I'm sorry, man."

Eric shrugs and stuffs his mouth full.

"It upsets him, so we usually don't talk about it," Mary tells him, her expression guarded.

None of us ever talks about Charlotte, North Carolina if we can help it. Too many bad memories all around.

"Cool." Ethan goes to steal another piece of bacon, and Eric's fork lands centimeters from his hand.

"Get your own."

"I'd share my bacon with you." He winks at Eric, and then this look of shock and a little horror flitters through his eyes.

"Here you can have mine." Mary shoves her plate at him, realizing like I do that Ethan likes Eric just as much and isn't ready to admit it either. At this rate, they'll both be married with kids before they're ready to admit the truth.

"Thanks, gorgeous." Ethan's smile turns flirty, which causes Eric to tense up, and Mary blatantly ignores Ethan.

"You done with your finals yet?" I ask to relieve some of the tension.

"Yup, I am officially a free man." He sits back and pops a piece of bacon in his mouth. "Is there anything better than bacon?"

"No," we all answer him. It's true. Everything is better with bacon.

"You going home for Christmas?"

"I was supposed to, but my dad got a work assignment, and he'll be out of the country until sometime in February. Mom went with him. I could go to my sister's, but I don't want to deal with a four-year-old who doesn't understand personal space. Don't get me wrong, I love the kid, but I can only deal with him in increments of five or ten minutes at a time."

"So what are you going to do?"

"Dunno yet. Probably crash at Wade's or Jordan's. Their parents are cool."

"Why don't you spend Christmas with us?" I put my glass of OJ down, aware of Eric's eyes snapping to me. "Me, Mary, and Eric are spending Christmas at my dad's. Zeke won't care if we bring along one more."

"Seriously?"

"Sure, you can even help us out if you want to, or you can lounge by the pool."

"Your dad has a pool?"

"Do you not know who Ezekiel Crane is?" Mary asks.

"Her dad?" Ethan's attention swivels between me and Mary and then to Eric, who looks ready to hurl all of a sudden. "Dude, you okay?"

"Fine." Eric takes several gulps of coffee. "I'm good."

"I'm surprised you don't know who he is." I pull his attention from Eric and back to me. "My dad's name is always bandied around when it comes to the occult. He's pretty big in the supernatural world."

"I may be the camera guy for The Ghost Chasers, but I honestly don't pay that much attention outside of editing. Wade probably knows who he is, but I don't."

"That's okay. You're less likely to be afraid of him, then." I flash him a smile.

APRYL BAKER

"He owns an old plantation right outside town, complete with pool and more guest rooms than he knows what to do with. We're having a party on Saturday night, though, so you'll need a tux."

"A tux? I don't own a tux."

"No worries, you can rent one. We're going shopping tomorrow for our dresses, and you and Eric can tag along to find a tux."

"Cool. What do you need help with? The show you're putting together?"

"Uh, Mattie's not doing that anymore. Mary and I are still gonna do something, but maybe not that particular kind of show."

"I, uh…" I clear my throat, nervous. "I don't normally tell strangers…"

"I'm not a stranger," Ethan cuts me off. "We're friends."

Which is true. He's become a regular among our movie nights and just hanging out in general.

"Which is why I want to tell you the truth." I take a deep breath and look around. The place is busy. A lot of the college crowd comes here, and this

128

morning is no different. "I need to go do some research when we leave here. If you want to come along, I'll tell you everything about me."

"Sure. I got nothing going on."

"You coming too, Eric? Mary has one more final before she can drag herself on to the hunt."

Eric nods, swallowing a little more loudly than he intended. I just thrust Ethan at him for the entirety of Christmas break. He'll be right there, up close and personal for weeks. Eric won't be able to hide from his feelings. Maybe this is a good thing, or maybe it's a bad thing.

Either way, I think both of them might have to come to terms with their feelings sooner than they want to. Or they'll continue blind as a bat or unwilling to admit it. I don't know if Ethan realizes how he feels, but maybe being around Eric all the time instead of just hanging out and then going home will help him with that.

I just hope it was a good idea.

I decided to pre-empt Zeke and go talk to Father David myself. He's my family's priest, but he never tries to pressure me about coming to mass, not the way Zeke or my grandparents do. It's probably why I like him so much.

His church sits on the very edge of the city. It's not some sweeping grand cathedral style church. Instead, it's a simple building—a parish church, if you will—with a few stained-glass windows. You would never think the Cranes would grace these humble walls with their presence, given their money and prestige, but to me, it's one of their redeeming qualities. When it comes to their religion, they're the ones who are humble.

"Why are we at your dad's church?" Eric shuts off the heat as soon as I pull up.

"Because I need information about The Red Church."

"What's that?"

"The Hathaway Foundation's first case." I get out and lock the car once Eric and Ethan have joined me. "I hope Father David can give me more information about it or put me in touch with someone who can."

"Why does that sound familiar?" Ethan mutters as he follows me up the steps and into the one-story building. Father David's office, as well as his living quarters, are off the main hall. The congregation bathroom, Sunday school room, and kitchen are on the other side. As far as I know, the congregation has never had any kind of dinner here, but they do cook for the homeless. I've helped out a couple times. Never told Zeke or Lila, though. I don't want them thinking I'm going to become Catholic, but what Father David does for the homeless is worthy of a few volunteers.

Eric shrugs. "I've never heard of it. Did you call and let Father David know we were coming?"

"Yeah, I texted him earlier."

"You and a priest are texting?" Eric quirks a brow. "I thought you hated Catholicism."

"I don't hate it. I just don't agree with certain things. I have a deep respect for religion, any religion. I may not agree with all its doctrines, but that doesn't mean I can't be friends with someone who does."

"You're friends with Father David now?"

"Yes." I turn to look at him. "What is your problem?"

"No problem." He cuts his eyes away from me, telling me there *is* a problem. He's probably mad I invited Ethan for Christmas. Tough. He'll deal with it or he won't.

Father David LaCroux appears before I can say anything else. He sees us standing near the entryway and hurries over. He's in his early fifties, maybe, but he still has a full head of dark red hair, and his blue eyes are always laughing. You'd think he was Irish and not French by looking at him.

"Emma, it's good to see you." The father hugs me and then waits for introductions. His manners are exceptional. Bet Lila wishes some of them would rub off on me.

"Father, you remember Eric, and this is our friend, Ethan. This is Father David LaCroux."

"Father," Ethan says and nods. "Nice to meet you."

Eric does this chin thrust thing that I think is meant to be a greeting.

"I have to say I was surprised you asked to come talk to me."

"I need some help, and I'm hoping you can do that for me or at least point me in the right direction."

"Of course. Let's go somewhere a little more comfortable, though."

Father David ushers us out of the church and to his private quarters. Once we're seated in his living room, which is very comfy with its soft couch and quaint tables, he sits in the chair across from us.

"Now, tell me, what do you need help with?"

"What can you tell me about The Red Church?"

His face goes from curious to alarmed to outright fear in less than three-point-five seconds.

"Why are you interested in that church property?"

"It's not church property, Father."

"Of course, it is. The church has owned it since it was built."

"Not anymore. It belongs to Kasey Jones now. He's wanting to build it out into a residential and commercial property."

"But…" Father David stands. "Excuse me for a moment. I need to make a call."

"What was that all about?" Ethan whispers when Father David leaves.

"I have no idea." Father David's reaction actually scared me. No one else's had, but a priest acting like I'd just told him the devil himself was sitting in a church pew did.

Father David leaves us sitting here a

good half hour before he reappears, his face pale and his hands more than a little shaky. He looks scared.

"Father?"

He sinks down into the armchair. "Emma, could I bother you to get me a glass of water, please?"

"Sure." I stand and go into the small kitchen right off the living room. I'd seen it when he brought us in earlier. Finding a clean glass in the drainer, I check the fridge for a bottle of water. I'm not one for tap water if it can be helped. Sure enough, I see a gallon of water sitting on the shelf and hastily pour him a glass. He doesn't look any better when I hand it to him a minute later.

"Thank you," he murmurs and takes several long drinks.

"Are you okay, Father? Do I need to call someone?"

"Someone should have called me," he says darkly and sets the glass down. "Emma, you need to promise me you won't go near that place."

"I can't, Father. I've already taken the job, and I don't break my word. What is wrong with it? First Mrs. Banks freaked out, and now you."

"What does your father say?"

"He told Kasey if he could get the place cleaned up, he'd invest in it. He wants it de-ghosted too."

"If only it were as simple as ghosts."

"Uh, isn't it?" I lean forward, curious. "I know about the massacre of 1812, and then about the nuns hanging themselves a few years later. I see why there'd be some pretty angry ghosts there, but I can help them."

Ethan makes a noise, and Eric kicks him. We'll fill him on my reaping abilities later. Right now, I'm more concerned with the look of utter terror stealing over every other expression on the good father's face.

"You may be able to help the ghosts, but you cannot help the evil that lives there, child. It is unholy."

"What evil?"

"This should never have happened. The Vatican wasn't aware of the auction until after it happened, and the owner wouldn't let them buy it back."

"Father David, you're not making sense."

He jumps up and starts to pace, muttering.

Eric leans over Ethan. "I think maybe we should call Zeke."

"I think you're right." I pull out my phone and do just that. He answers on the first ring.

"Emma?"

"Hey, Papa. I think you better come over to Father David's. He might be having a nervous breakdown."

"What?" Something falls, and Zeke ignores it. "Are you there with him?"

"Yeah. I came to ask him about The Red Church, and he went postal."

"That doesn't sound…I'll be there as soon as I can. Try to calm him down if you can."

"I don't think there is any calming him down."

"Do what you can, *ma petite*. I'll be there soon."

Once I put my phone back in my pocket, I watch Father David pace, muttering in a language I don't know. I get up and approach him as slowly as I would a wild animal. "Father, please come sit down. You're working yourself up, and Zeke said your heart isn't as well as it used to be. You need to try to calm down." Zeke's been really worried about him since he had a heart attack last year.

He shakes his head but doesn't resist me when I lead him back to the chair he'd vacated.

"I called Papa. He'll be here soon."

"Your father doesn't understand what's there, what lives on those lands. You can't go there, child, especially after dark. Promise me you won't."

I never make a promise I can't keep, so I don't this time either.

Father David sighs loudly. "You just don't understand."

"Then make me understand."

"It's an ancient evil, one as old as the Earth itself. Created in the shadows of the darkness before God created light."

"A primordial evil?" Ethan asks. "Those are just rumors, Father."

"No, son, people have forgotten what lives in the dark. Even the Bible says if you knew what was in the dark, you wouldn't go out into the night. With modern technology, people's fears have diminished. But that doesn't mean the evil has diminished. It grows stronger in the lack of faith most have these days. It feeds right in front of us."

"What's a primordial evil?" Eric looks as confused as I feel, so I'm glad he asked.

"You understand the concept of good and evil, light and dark? One cannot exist without the other. A primordial evil is something that was created in the beginning, something so dark that only the light of goodness could beat it back. When God created the light that shines in our world, it drove the evil into the very darkest of holes and kept it there. But sometimes, that evil escapes its prison."

"And whatever lives on the church grounds is one of these dark creatures?" Eric frowns.

"Not just something. It's one of the first creatures that came into existence when the dark ruled and the light was just a whisper, told to terrify their most unruly."

"I didn't feel anything like that when I was there."

"You've been there? That means it has your scent." He looks so upset, I reach over and take his hand.

"When I was there, I didn't feel anything like you're describing. I felt the Loa and a few ghosts who seemed more than a little frightened."

"The Loa would have tried to warn you away." Father David nods, speaking more to himself than us. "They protect that land, keep the truly innocent away."

"You believe in the Loa?" Eric arches a brow. "Isn't it against your religion or something to acknowledge other gods?"

"The Loa aren't gods," Father David says. "They are spirits that roam the Earth, spirits that are neither good nor bad, they just are. I may not call upon them, but I don't doubt their existence."

Mind. Blown.

Maybe there's more to Father David than I'd originally thought.

"Josiah told me once that true magic is neither good nor evil, but a culmination of the two. That's what it sounds like you're describing with the Loa."

Father David turns his head my way. "There are many things about this world we don't understand, Emma. Supernatural things included. The Bible says suffer not a witch to live, but I know people who use magic to do good things. I would suffer to allow those people to live and continue to do good things. Be that right or wrong, I don't know. It's something I'll discuss with my maker when I die. Until then, all I can do is what I believe is the right thing, what keeps the most people safe. What I can do and still look at myself in the mirror every day."

"People like Papa."

He gives me a sad smile. "Your father does many things that could be looked upon as evil, but sometimes those things allow him to bring about kindness and true purity. Who am I to condemn him in one breath and then hold out my other hand for the many blessings he has graced this small parish with?"

"But you give him absolution when he

confesses, don't you?"

"For the sins he confesses, yes, but I wonder how much he holds back. But that will be between him and God one day."

"You're not at all like I thought you were."

Now, that earns me a real smile.

"I'm not the old guard of the church. Many of the newer priests have different opinions on the scripture and how literally to take it."

"But you believe in this primordial evil thing, though?"

The anxiousness flows back into his expression. "Yes, Emma. I firmly believe in it. I was tasked to protect the people of New Orleans from it."

"You still haven't said what it is, though, not really."

The knock at the door interrupts us. "That'll be your father. Excuse me while I get the door."

"This just got a thousand times more interesting," Ethan whispers when Father David leaves the room. His eyes are shining with excitement, but I can guarantee mine aren't.

In fact, I'm beginning to think maybe I should refund Kasey.

But he'll just go hire other people.

People who will die.

And I can't have that on my conscience, so as uneasy as I am, I have to see this through.

No matter what's waiting for me.

Zeke is wearing a three-piece suit when he walks through the door, looking thoroughly out of place in the priest's simple surroundings. Crap on toast. I probably pulled him out of an important meeting, but I wasn't sure what to do. Father David was falling apart, and I had no clue how to help him. Zeke is good in these kinds of situations. He assures me I will be too, but I have my doubts. I hate conflict. I used to thrive on it. In fact, I used to do everything I could to make trouble, but since my soul was shattered, I'm different. More grown up, sure, but also less likely to start a fight. I'll finish one, mind you, but nine times out of ten,

I keep my nose clean these days.

Part of it's fear. I know that. I've talked about it with my therapist. I'm afraid of what I can do. Maybe when I grow comfortable with my gifts, some of that fear will go away. But part of it's also Dan. I'm afraid one day I'll do something so bad, he'll walk away from me. I couldn't survive if he left me, so I'm trying to postpone that day for as long as I can.

"You have to keep her away from there," Father David says as he follows my dad into the room. "It's too dangerous, even for her."

"There are things you don't know about *ma petite*, Father, things you'll never know. But it's those things that keep her safe. I'm confident she can handle anything that church throws at her."

"Not this." Father David turns and heads out of the room.

"Has he been this upset for long?" Zeke sits down in one of the two armchairs.

"Since I mentioned The Red Church."

"I have no idea why he's reacting this way. Or why Mrs. Banks did either."

"He won't tell me what's there, only that it's a primordial evil."

"What?" Zeke's blue eyes flare with shock. "Did he say which one?"

"Nope." Ethan leans back, his shoulder brushing Eric's. Eric leans forward in response.

"Papa, you remember Ethan, don't you? He's going to be staying with us over Christmas. He has nowhere else to go."

Zeke's eyes flash up and zero in on Eric. I'm not the only one who's guessed how he feels about Ethan.

"Is that so?" Zeke asks this more to Eric than to anyone else. Leave it to my papa to make sure Eric's okay with it. He thinks of Mary and Eric as his own, though. He'll protect them same as he does me.

"Yeah." Eric nods, understanding Zeke's asking him if he's okay with it. I think he and Papa may have had a few conversations about his feelings toward the male population. Eric's ghost settled in my ex-boyfriend's body. Jake, much to our astonishment, liked guys. It explained so much. The boy never pushed me for sex while we were together. Which was odd for a teenage boy. I think the old Jake hid his real feelings out of fear. There are still too many homophobes in the world. I wish people would just realize love is love and it shouldn't be judged.

"I hope you don't mind, sir." Ethan sits up straight, and I hide a grin. I think my father intimidates him, and he does his best to not show it while actually doing just the opposite.

"No, I don't mind." Zeke turns his attention back to me. "Did you feel anything strange when you inspected the property?"

"Simon was there, so I didn't really have the chance to fully inspect it, but no. I got nothing weird or even remotely evil from it. That may change when I go back, though."

"I'm beginning to wonder if you shouldn't go back."

"I can't let him bring other people in to

die, Papa."

"You were already thinking this is a bad idea, *oui*?"

I nod, troubled. I think it's an epically *bad* idea, but I one I have to see through. "I can't walk away from it, Papa. You know I can't."

"You and your sense of duty and morality." Zeke shakes his head. "I wish I had gotten to you sooner, and then I might have prevented this save the world complex you are cursed with."

Father David bustles in with a bottle of what I think is whiskey and a tray of five tumblers.

"If we are going to discuss this, we need a little fortification."

"We're not twenty-one yet, Father," I tell him.

"I am," Ethan says.

"Trust me, Emma, you're going to need this." He pours a good amount into each one and then hands them out. I set mine on the coffee table. I don't drink. Never have, never will. Eric, I notice, sets his down as well. He drinks, but not often. Mostly at his frat parties, and even then, it's minimal. Ethan, however, is a party boy. He's not afraid of booze, and I've seen him inhale more than his fair share. But he only does that at parties. He doesn't get lit every day. I'd call him your average college student still trying to figure things out on his own.

"Father, what has you so worked up?" Zeke drowns his liquor in one long swallow. My throat aches thinking about the burn that would cause.

"Can I not sway you to stay away from there?" Father David asks me.

"No. I can't let someone else walk in there and die. I would never forgive myself, knowing I might have been able to prevent it."

"She definitely doesn't get her sense of right and wrong from you," Father David tells Zeke, a rueful smile toying with his lips.

"Give me time, Father, I'm working on it."

"No, Ezekiel, leave the girl be. Her morality is part of the shield that protects her."

"I never thought of that."

Father David nods and downs his own drink. He quickly pours himself another. "If I can't persuade you to leave it, then I have to tell you what you're facing."

Which is what I've been trying to get him to do since he started babbling about a primordial evil.

"Have you ever heard of the rumors that surround the Ursuline Convent?"

Zeke gasps. "You swore to me they were just rumors, David."

"I'm sworn to protect those secrets." He straightens. "Part of that is convincing others they *are* just rumors."

"I could have helped you protect them."

"You would have found a way to manipulate that help, and you know it."

Of that, I have no doubts. My father is not a nice man. He loves me and I him, but I'm not blind to his many faults. He has no qualms about doing anything and everything to get what he wants.

"Someone want to let us in on the secret?" Nathan asks, effectively interrupting Zeke and Father David's glaring match.

Father David sighs and runs a hand through his thinning hair. His scalp is peeking through a patch on the top of his head. I hope to God my hair never decides to do that. My hair is my one vanity. It's unruly most days, the curls frizzing up in the heat and humidity, but I'd cry if anything ever happened to it.

"You're sure I can't talk you out of going back?"

"No, Father. I made a commitment."

Another long sigh escapes him. "Then you must understand what it is you are facing. Do you know very much about the history of New Orleans?"

"You know I didn't grow up here, Father, and I haven't really done that much research into the city's history. I'm thinking I need to make that a priority."

"Given your unique gifts, Emma, I would suggest you do that sooner rather than later." Father David takes a deep breath. "Back when New Orleans was a struggling colony of France, the female population was sparse. So the colony officials wrote to the king, asking for him to send over suitable young ladies to help populate the colony. The women who came over were housed at the Ursuline Convent until such a time a proper suitor could be found for them."

"While that sounds very feudal, it's not supernatural." I cross my legs, impatient to hear the meat of the story.

"The girls were secretly called The Casket Girls."

Well, now, that's a little more supernatural.

"Why?"

"They arrived with a casket carrying their belongings. Those caskets were stored on the third floor of the convent until the girls were betrothed."

"They came with actual coffins?" Eric asks, propping his elbows on his knees. "Real caskets? Like a vampire or something?"

"Or something," Father David mutters.

Zeke makes this humming noise, and I glance at him. His gaze is riveted to the good father.

"When one of the nuns went upstairs to collect a young woman's things from one such casket, she found it empty. She found them all empty. Scared, she called for the priest, who summoned the archdiocese. What happened after that is not well known."

"But you know the truth."

The father nods, his expression becoming distant. None of us push him to speak. Sometimes the truths that need to come to light are ones that should never see the stark light of reality. Some things need to stay dead and buried. I have a feeling this is one of those things.

"I was told the truth when I received my parish here. It took me weeks to come to terms with what I learned, but I have never failed in my duties, not once, but I cannot protect against what I do not know is coming."

"You mean the auction?" Zeke guessed.

"Yes. Some accountant decided to put the land up for sale, as it was a prime piece of real estate that netted the church millions of dollars. He failed to check the code beside the property, the code that said under no circumstances was that property to ever be sold. It is an unfortunate side effect of having someone besides our own handle certain aspects of church business."

Which is part of the reason I resist my family's attempts at converting me to Catholicism. It's as much a business as it is a religion.

"What is that they wanted to protect?" I ask.

"You misunderstand. The archdiocese wished to protect the people of New Orleans from what they discovered in those caskets." Father David takes several deep breaths. "The caskets were empty that evening, and a deep fear took root in the good sisters, the priest, and the archdiocese. They waited in a small room beneath the stairs for morning to come. They heard the floorboards creaking a few minutes before dawn, the feet climbing the stairs."

"Was it the girls who had arrived?"

"No. Those girls were safely in their rooms. They had no knowledge of what came from France with them."

"Then who did they hear?" Ethan's eyes are lit up with excitement. He's been around Wade and the Ghost Chasers too long.

"They waited for the sun to be high in the sky before they dared go upstairs. The coffins were exactly as they'd been left, only they were no longer empty. Inside were creatures. They appeared human, or some of them did. Others had a monstrous visage. Their faces were smeared with a red substance, and the priest and the archdiocese representative fled, sure they'd found the source of the infant mortality rate that had skyrocketed since the arrival of the women from France."

"Infants?" I whispered, horror starting to rise as my mind worked through what was actually in those coffins.

"The archdiocese ordered the room sealed. Precautions were put in place, down to blessed nails that were used to seal the shutters on the third floor of the convent. No one was allowed to go near the back stairwell. The door leading into the entrance of the third floor was nailed shut, the nails blessed as well. Rumors say the Pope himself blessed the screws that went into place, but that is not the case. Perhaps if he had, what eventually happened would not have."

"You're talking about vampires, aren't you?"

Father David's gaze collides with mine.

"No, Emma, I'm talking about the creatures that *created* vampires."

Fudgepops.

I swallow past the lump that has formed and won't go away.

"As I said, there were several human-looking creatures in those coffins. They would be the children of the monsters in the others. The primordial blood demon, as we call them, have no sense of morality or of mercy or goodness. They are cold, calculated creatures of pure evil. They feed on the blood of the innocent, and what is more innocent than a baby?"

Up until now, Zeke had been quiet, but not anymore.

"Emma Rose, you are not going anywhere near that place."

"Papa, let him finish his story before you go all Neanderthal on me."

His nostrils flare, and I can tell he's about to argue. "Don't you want to know how the story moves from the convent to the church?"

He's as much a sucker for a good story as I am. As horrified as I am, this is still a story worth listening to.

Father David continues when Zeke begrudgingly retakes his seat.

"In 1812, New Orleans was invaded. Rumors ran rampant by then of the sealed third floor, and the convent was invaded because of it. Convinced treasures were up there, the invaders broke through the doors and into the arms of the waiting creatures who had not fed since they'd been sealed in that room. They massacred many that night, including everyone at what is known now as The Red Church. It held the most church officials within easy access, and the creatures wanted revenge. What happened to those poor people...I can't even imagine the terror they felt."

"Then how were they locked away again?" I ask.

"Sunlight was their one weakness.

They fled back to their coffins as the first rays of the sun crested the skyline. The archdiocese sent a delegation to the convent and the abbey that morning. They dealt with the dead and resealed the room at the convent. Only there was one problem. One of the coffins remained empty. Warnings were sent out to the hunters of old, and the countryside was scoured."

"But you didn't find it?"

The father shakes his head. "No. We searched for many years before the hunt was given up. The Vatican moved more nuns and a priest back into the old abbey. They were not told of the creatures locked away within the convent. They should have been, and perhaps if they had been, another tragedy may have been preventable."

The nuns who committed suicide. I remember Simon telling me about that.

"It was shortly after the Christmas Eve mass that the creature struck. It slaughtered them all. We told the people that there was a mass suicide. After what happened in 1812, the church feared letting them know the truth. Two nights later, the creature appeared at the convent, asking to meet with whoever was holding its brethren hostage."

"It showed up at the convent?" Eric's eyes widened. He seemed as enthralled with the story as Ethan.

"Yes. A bargain was struck that night between the church and the creature."

"Why didn't the creature just kill them?"

Father David smiles slightly. "Hunters had put a protection circle around the convent. The creature could not pass."

"Smart."

"Indeed, Emma, it was very smart. Unfortunately, the hunters couldn't do the same for all of New Orleans, and the church was forced to make a compromise. The blessed nails were to be removed from the shutters, and should some unsuspecting person come to close to the walls, the creatures could feed if they could convince them to come inside."

"I thought they fed on infants?" Zeke leans over and picks up the bottle of liquor and pours himself a healthy dose.

"They are very persuasive." Father David holds out his own glass, and Zeke refills it. "They convinced people to bring them infants, and if that failed, they fed upon whoever came close enough. The protection circled extended five feet in front of the gates. It gave them room to jump the wall and pull the unsuspecting person inside. Some mornings, they found the dead bodies of infants. Those were buried around the church walls. The bodies of the adult were burned."

"They buried the babies at the wall? Why not give them a proper burial?" This seems even more horrific to me than the creatures themselves. Those poor babies deserved to be put to rest properly.

"There were many superstitions back then, Emma. It may have been they feared the bodies were marked with evil and therefore unclean. They wouldn't have been allowed on consecrated ground."

"That's awful."

"Yes, it is, and when the new walls went up, that was rectified. The bones of over a hundred infants were found. Once the police were done with their investigation, they were given a proper burial."

"How did they explain that, though?" I ask.

"The police chief knew what they would find. From the beginning, the authorities in town knew what was housed in the convent. The bones were seen to quickly because of that."

"At least they were finally put to rest peacefully," I mutter.

"It was a consequence of the time, Emma. The same way suicides were not allowed on consecrated ground until the Pope reversed that decree in 1983. Superstition is as much a part of religion as anything else."

I stare him down. He and I will never agree on this. I respect him and all he does, but I'm not a Catholic and therefore am not required to defend the institution.

"The research team that died outside the walls, was that the creatures as well?" Zeke reaches for my untouched glass and downs it. Zeke rarely drinks this much. I may end up having to drive him home unless his driver is with him today.

"Yes. It was a death that couldn't be hidden. Too many people knew they were setting up shop to see if the rumors about vampires were true. They tried to wait inside the walls, and when denied, they camped outside the walls. From what I was told, the nuns did their best to keep watch, but they failed."

"You're not going there, *ma petite*. I forbid it." Zeke's normally warm blue eyes are darker, colder. He means business. I ignore him.

"Father, the deal that was made, did it include the creature outside the protection circle, or was it left unchecked?"

"We didn't know where it slept during the day. The truth is we still don't, but that didn't stop us from trying to keep it contained. Another protection ring was put around the Red Church's property line. It's been reinforced once in the mid-fifties, but we think the creature lives within the circle. The mass slaughter stopped soon after. No one has been on those grounds since the day the protection circle was created. Not even the hunters who reinforced it. They stayed well outside the circle."

"The protection circle still stands, then?"

"I don't know. I will have to contact the local hunters…"

"I'll do that. Cass is already working with me to de-ghost the place."

"No, not the Willows. They do not know of the creatures. Emmet Wallace will deal with the circle. It is his family blood that went into the creation of the circle, and his family's blood that must be used to maintain it."

"Be that as it may, if Kasey brings in his construction crews, they are going to break ground for all the buildings he has plans for."

"I will try to purchase the property from him," Zeke says. "If I offer him enough money, he'll sell."

"No, Papa, I don't think he will. This is about more than money for him. It's about proving to his father he can do this. Pride gets in the way of common sense most days."

"I'll still try."

And I know he will, but I don't think Kasey will budge.

"Wait, I have a question." Ethan tilts his head, thinking. "Why did you remove the blessed nails when you trapped the other creature behind the protection circle? I mean, if it couldn't do what it said, why not keep the other creatures locked up?"

"In the supernatural community, when you do not honor your word, it means death." Zeke centers his attention on Ethan. "Had the Church reneged on the deal, there would have been serious consequences. The creature itself might not have been able to retaliate, but it would have gotten word to others who would have come after all of the priests and the nuns. It's how it works in the world of the supernatural. It's one of our most basic covenants. One even the Church respects."

We say our goodbyes soon after that, Father David assuring us he'll get in touch with Emmet Wallace. I make a note to ask Cass about the guy. I've never heard of him, but then again, the only hunters in New Orleans I know are the Willows.

Zeke thankfully has his own driver, and I promise not to go near the church until after he tries to buy it from Kasey. That is a promise I can keep because I know someone who might know a little about the situation, or at least could find out.

A supernatural Historian in the form of Heather Malone.

I know she'll help me, even if talking to me hurts us both.

And to keep people safe, I'll bite the bullet and deal with the pain Heather brings.

Eric and Ethan are more than happy to follow me back to my dorm room. We'd called Cass and asked him to swing by as well. He is so gonna flip his lid when he finds out this was kept from him. It shouldn't have been hidden from the hunters. I'm not even sure how it was kept a secret. Given the rumors, a hunter must have gotten a little curious at some point. So why didn't they know about the highly dangerous creature in their own back yard?

"Okay, time to 'fess up." Ethan drops down on the couch in the living area between my and Mary's room. "I knew you knew more about the supernatural than you let on."

"I don't normally tell anyone what I can do, so I expect you to keep this to yourself. No telling Wade anything."

"He's still pissed you had him thrown off the property the one and only time we worked together."

"Well, we didn't actually work together. I helped out Doc."

"Another bone of contention with him. Dr. Olivet is his idol, and the guy all but treated him like a child playing ghost hunter."

"You *are* children playing ghost hunters," I say, "and eventually it's going to catch up with you. Ghosts are dangerous and not to be messed with."

"They're harmless," he argues.

"That's what I used to think too, but it's not the case. I had no idea they could hurt you until Mirror Boy caused me to have a seizure." I refrain from mentioning Eric is Mirror Boy. That's his truth to tell. "Then I had a soul eater almost kill me by draining my energy to the point I was so weak, I couldn't defend myself."

"How did you?" Ethan leans forward and accepts the cold bottle of water Eric offers him as he too sits down. He tosses one my way as well.

"This is the part where you have to promise me you'll keep what I tell you secret. It's important, Ethan. You can't tell anyone."

He nods.

"No, you have to say the words."

"She's right," Eric tells him. "You have to say the words. She's about to trust you with something important because you're our friend. We need to hear you say the words."

"I promise I won't tell anyone. You can trust me. I like you guys a lot, and you're important to me. Eric and I are super bros, and you and Mary, well, I'd never do anything that could harm either of you or cause you pain. I swear."

I smile at his heartfelt words. I already know everything he just said about him, but it's important for him to say it. When you speak the words, they become more than just an empty promise. They become truth.

"Now, back to your question of how I survived. I had help. I reaped a ghost, and their energy gave me the strength to deal with Jonas."

"What do you mean, you reaped a ghost?"

"You know what reapers are?"

"Like the grim reaper?"

"Sort of. Reapers are tasked with escorting ghosts to the other side after they die. They appear as a loved one or someone important to the individual to make it easier for them to cross over."

Ethan nods. "Makes sense. You hear all kinds of stories about people who almost died or on the verge of dying and claim they see their loved ones."

"It's not really their family, though. It's a reaper."

He tilts his head, thinking, and then his eyes widen. "Hold up, you said *you* reaped a ghost...?"

Eric grins, waiting for me to tell Ethan the truth. It's hard to swallow, but as much as Ethan is into the supernatural, he might take to it easier than most. We'll see.

"I'm what's called a living reaper," I explain. "I died when I was five, but the paramedics were able to revive me. When I woke up, I could see ghosts. My death activated my reaping abilities, and I do what I can to help the ghost move on. When I die, I'll become a full-fledged reaper."

Ethan stares at me, unblinking. I can't tell what he's thinking. His expression is blank. He turns toward Eric.

"It's the truth. She's not pulling your leg."

"That's the coolest freaking thing I've ever heard." The awe in his voice inspires a round of laughter from Eric. "Dude, don't be laughing. Your sister is a reaper."

"She *is* the coolest person ever, but what she does can be downright scary at times." He sobers with his words. "Ghosts are lost souls, wandering this plane of existence, afraid, alone, and not understanding they're dead. Some can even be tricksters, and some try to help the living, but after a while, it wears on them. They grow angry and more afraid than confused. Those emotions turn to rage, and then they go crazy. It's those ghosts you have to worry about because they have enough kinetic energy to manipulate objects, and when they gain that ability, hurting someone is as easy for them as breathing to you and me."

"You sound like you know a lot about ghosts," Ethan says, a speculative look in his eyes.

"More than I want to."

The wealth of pain in his voice speaks to his past, a past Ethan may never know about.

"Are you like her? Can you see ghosts too?"

"I can, but I'm not a reaper."

Now, that's news to me. He never talks about any leftover ghost energy he took with him into Jake's body. Why didn't he ever tell me?

"I can't talk to them, not like Hathaway can, but I can see them. It's not a fun thing to turn around and see a mangled corpse staring at you. I've screamed like a girl on more than one occasion. I also don't talk about it, so I'm not answering all those questions I can see rattling around in your head."

"It's cool." Ethan sits back. "You'll tell me more when you're ready. I can wait you out."

I quirk a brow at him, and he winks at me. I wish I knew how he felt about Eric. Sometimes, like now, I think he cares deeply, but other times, he's just the super bro he says he is. It confuses me, so I know it has to confuse Eric just as much.

Eric crosses his arms, a defensive posture I've come to recognize. It's not even his. Jake used to do that whenever he got nervous about something. I think a lot of Jake's memories are still in there, locked away, but sometimes they leak out. One day, Eric might have to deal with all of Jake's memories, and I don't know how he'll react when whatever door those memories are behind opens up.

Jake's parents would be grateful, I think. Eric remembers nothing of Jake, and if he could access those memories, he'd be able to fit more fully into the

Owens' family. Not that they haven't accepted him. They have, especially Mrs. Owens, but Eric holds himself back the tiniest bit because he sort of feels like they love the shell he's inhabiting and not him.

Which is not true. Mrs. Owens knows Eric isn't Jake, and she loves him. I've seen it firsthand. She recognized the lost soul he is and took him in. She doesn't compare him to Jake either. She accepts Eric as is.

Mr. Owens holds out hope that his son will eventually regain his memories and be the old Jake. It's part of why Eric came to school down here. He hates to cause the man who took him in any pain. Maybe if those memories come back, the two of them can come to the same kind of relationship Eric has with his mother.

But all that is a problem for another day.

"The same goes for what Eric just told you," I tell Ethan. "You can't tell anyone about what he can do."

"I would never."

"Good. Now, how are you with

173

research?"

"Research?" He makes a face like I've just asked him to eat boogers or something. "Why?"

"Because I need you and Eric to head into town and visit the library. Look through the old newspaper files about anything having to do with the convent and The Red Church."

"What will you be doing?" Eric asks, looking uncomfortable.

"Talking to Heather."

He winces. He knows how much that will hurt.

"I don't know, Hathaway, maybe Mary or I should do it…"

"No," I cut him off, "I'll do it. We'll meet at Zeke's tonight and compare notes. Tomorrow, we install the cameras and the mics. Hopefully, we'll capture the creature on video and maybe even see where its hiding place is."

"I highly doubt it's sleeping in the church itself."

"You never know, Eric. It could have dug a hole underneath the church. It could have an entire basement dug under that place."

"Please don't tell me we're going to be searching for hidden entrances."

"You know we will."

He groans. "I should have gone home for Christmas."

"Nah, then you'd miss seeing me for two whole weeks." Ethan winks at Eric, who blushes and gets up. He mumbles something neither of us understands. I'm not sure Ethan even realizes what he said, but if he does, he doesn't say anything.

"Dude, you are not that awesome," Eric finally says. "I wouldn't miss you at all."

"I call BS," Ethan says and laughs. "Super bros always miss each other." He holds out his hand, and Eric, like the super bro he is, doesn't leave him hanging. He bumps his fist against Ethan's.

"Super bros to the end, man." Eric throws his empty water bottle in the trash. "I got to get going. I got to call my mom and then pack up. If you're coming to Zeke's, you need to pack too."

"Of course, I'm coming. I've heard all

of you guys talk about Mrs. Banks and her amazing cooking. Think I'd pass up the chance to test it out myself?"

"You'll gain ten pounds before Christmas dinner. Expect another fifteen during the dinner."

Ethan rubs his stomach and sighs. "Can't wait. We'll head to the library when Eric finishes his phone call. See you later, Ghost Girl."

"Don't call her that," Eric says, his voice hard. "She hates that nickname."

"Noted." Ethan shoots me an apologetic smile. "Sorry, Em."

"No worries." I wave his apology off. "See you guys later."

Once the door is closed, I stare at my phone.

I don't want to do this, but I have to.

Taking a deep breath, I find her name in my contact list and hit the little phone icon to dial Heather Malone.

She picks up on the fourth ring.

"Mattie, honey? Are you okay? Is Dan okay?"

The Malones don't call me Emma either, and I never insisted they do. I'm Mattie to them. It's what Eli called me.

"I'm fine, and so is Dan."

"Thank goodness." Heather lets out a huge sigh. I can imagine her standing by her kitchen sink, clutching it with one hand and her phone in the other, taking several deep breaths to calm down.

"Sorry, I didn't mean to scare you."

"It's fine, honey. It's just…"

"Whenever I'm around, people tend to get hurt," I finish for her.

"That wasn't what I was going to say. Or at least not in those words."

See? She knows me too well. If it weren't for me, Eli would still be alive. It's something that will haunt me until the day I die. Heather may have forgiven me, but I'll never forgive myself. I know it wasn't my fault. It was a stupid curse, but if I'd never met him, I wouldn't be the reason he died.

"I know you wouldn't put it so bluntly, and I don't care that was your first thought, because it's true. There are usually bodies left in my wake. But I am sorry that's the first thought you have when it comes to me."

"No, honey, don't think like that. You never asked for what happened. You did everything you could to prevent it, to keep people safe. That's what you should remember."

I smile, knowing she can't see me. It's the mother in her that always tries to make me feel better. Sometimes she does, but most times she doesn't.

"Anyway, I'm hoping you can help me with something."

"If I can."

"I got asked to help clear out a property of the ghosts haunting it. Our first job as The Hathaway Foundation. Only we discovered the real problem wasn't ghosts. It's something called a primordial evil."

Heather swears. This lovely woman who I have never heard curse once lets out a string of curse words that would make the devil blush.

"Do you know what type?"

"Father David said it was a blood demon."

"Father David...Mattie, what property are you clearing?"

"It's known to the locals as The Red Church."

"I...why would the church ask you to go anywhere near that place?"

"They didn't. Father David didn't even know it had sold at auction. The new owner asked us to help him. He thinks it's just ghosts."

"The property sold? Who would have sold it knowing what's there?"

Well, she obviously knows about the

place, so that's good. Maybe I'll get answers sooner rather than later.

"It was an accountant who didn't check the code listed beside the property. He just saw a very valuable piece of land sitting stagnant and thought to make a quick profit for the church."

"Who bought it?"

"A developer."

I don't have to be standing in front of her to know her face paled.

"He can't break the protection seal…it can't get out."

"You know about The Red Church, then?"

"Yes," she whispers. "I made sure to acquaint myself with everything having to do with Louisiana and New Orleans specifically when you and Dan went there after the funeral. I needed to be armed with information. I'd lost one son, and I wasn't about to lose another because I didn't know what was waiting for him."

I am silent for so long, she must have realized what her words meant to me.

"Mattie, honey, I didn't mean you…I

was referring to the supernatural world down there."

She may deny it, but she did mean me. I'm probably going to be the one to get him killed someday.

"It doesn't really matter what you meant. I just need to know what you do about the events surrounding The Red Church. I don't trust the church to tell me everything."

She's quiet for a heartbeat, but then she picks back up. "The church is notorious for keeping its secrets close to its vest. If we hadn't had an Historian in the Vatican back in the day, we wouldn't know what we do."

"There were Historians inside the church?" That surprises me.

"There are *still* Historians inside the church. Not everyone believes the church has a right to keep secrets from us, and we do what we can to make sure those secrets don't stay hidden. At least not the ones involving the supernatural."

"You don't know how happy it makes me to realize there are people keeping a close eye on them. I know the church today isn't the same as it was, but there are still those who firmly believe that its secrets need to stay hidden."

"I'm right there with you. James is Catholic, and he takes the boys to church, but I'm not. I do go with them on holidays, but I grew up in the Holiness church."

"The holy rollers."

She laughs. "Yes, they can be quite loud when they get infused with the Holy Ghost, but they feel more real to me than a lot of others. I'm not big on their screaming and shouting, though. It's like they're putting on a show for their audience and not for God."

"Yup, right there with you. It's part of the reason I don't go to church myself. I haven't found one I'm comfortable with. I want to be able to go in my jeans and not feel like people are staring at me. Church shouldn't be about what you're wearing, but about why you're there."

"Exactly. That's how my church was growing up. You could come dressed in your Sunday best or in jeans and t-shirt, and you were welcomed."

"Back to The Red Church, can you email me anything about it? I have Eric and Ethan doing research at the library, but I don't know if they'll find anything of value." I go on to tell her what Father David told us. "I'm not sure if he left anything out or if his superiors kept things from him, but I need to know everything if I'm going to go up against this thing."

"Honey, that's not a good idea. There's a reason hunters have agreed for over a hundred years to leave the creature be behind a protective barrier. It's too dangerous."

"Zeke's trying to convince the guy to let him buy it. If that happens, he'll put up a security fence about twenty feet high around it with cameras. Nothing will get in or out. But if he can't convince Kasey to sell, Kasey will just go hire crews from out of town, and people might die, Heather. I can't be responsible for any more deaths if I can prevent them."

She's wise enough to not try and talk me out of my guilt. Something Dan still tries to do. I have to deal with it in my own time and in my own way.

"Okay, honey. It's going to take me a couple of hours. I'll scan everything I can for you, and what I don't have on hand, I'll write it down. Will that work?"

"I'm just shocked you gave up so easily on getting me to stay away."

"Because I know what it's like," she says. "I'm an Historian. We go into dangerous situations to chronicle the events that take place. If someone were to tell me I couldn't go, I might take their head off even though I know they mean well."

I guess maybe she does understand.

"Thanks, Heather."

"You're very welcome, Mattie. I do expect a full accounting of what happened, though. In writing."

"Sure thing." I smile, knowing it's the Historian in her that's demanding it. Same as whatever it is in me that demands I help people springs up when necessary. "And, Heather, merry Christmas."

"Merry Christmas to you too. We'll talk soon, honey."

Once she hangs up, I put my phone on the charger and look toward the open suitcase on the floor and my bed. I need to pack, but I need to nap too. Getting up early is not my thing. It's why I do my best to make sure none of my classes start before ten in the morning.

The packing can wait. I need to sleep more than I need to pile clothes into a suitcase.

I'm not sure what it is that wakes me, but I feel unsettled. Sitting up in bed, I listen to the quiet of the night. Something isn't right. I'm not sure what is wrong, but I cannot shake the sensation. I can't catch my breath, and my hands begin to shake as I sit here in the darkness, listening for something I know deep in my heart has come here to do harm.

I sit there for the longest time, unmoving, but when I do manage to shake free of this irrational fear, I get out of bed and put on my slippers, wrapping my dressing gown around my small frame. I creep to the door and listen, but I'm met with nothing but silence.

The door squeaks when I crack it the tiniest bit, but the hallway is pitch black. None of the candles are left burning at night. It's seen as a waste. I do not necessarily disagree, but in this one moment, I wish we were not so frugal with our candles. The darkness outside my room is thick and heavy, and I sense something out there. Light would be much welcomed within the hallway tonight.

Deciding to light my own candlestick, I hope Father Dougal doesn't quarrel at me on the morrow. Perhaps even he has awakened with this sense of impending dread.

I ease my door open and step outside, my solitary candle casting a meager glow around me. My free hand clutches at my rosary, a silent prayer going above. Something is not right here, and I hold to my faith to bolster my courage as I take a tentative step toward Sister Annalyn's chamber. There are not many nuns here, only seven of us, as well as Father Dougal and our Mother Superior.

Knocking upon Sister Annalyn's door

as quietly as I can, I whisper, "Sister Annalyn? Are you awake?"

The door is pulled open so quickly, I falter back, not expecting it. Sister Annalyn stands there, clutching her own rosary. Her expression is as fearful as mine.

"Do you feel it, Sister?" she whispers. "I cannot shake this horrible feeling of wrongness."

"I do. It woke me. Come, let us check on the others."

Sister Annalyn nods and fetches her own dressing gown. I feel exposed standing here alone in the hallway, but there is nothing that I can see to be afraid of. Just the heavy, thick darkness wrapping itself around us.

I shake myself out of my morbid thoughts when Sister Annalyn joins me. It is best not to dwell on things we cannot see. I hold my rosary tighter as the two of us wander down the hall, finding empty beds where our sisters should be slumbering after our Christmas Eve mass.

"Where are they?" Sister Annalyn

worries. Like me, this oppressive darkness is getting to her. She keeps looking up and down the hall, but my one candle is no match for it.

"I do not know, Sister. Perhaps they went to Mother Superior with their own fears. Come, let us find her and hope that is where our other sisters have disappeared to."

We make our way back to the center of the hallway where the circular staircase rests. Father Dougal and Mother Superior's bedchambers are the very top of the stairwell along with a spare bedroom, should we have important guests stay here.

Halfway up the flight of stairs, I pause. Sister Annalyn frowns, having heard it too.

There.

A whimper.

We take a few more steps up the stairs, and the sound reaches us again. Someone is in pain. My first thought is to run up the stairs and attempt to help, but something holds me back. It keeps me quiet. I lay a finger against Sister

189

Annalyn's lips when she starts to say something. This isn't right. Whatever is in the abbey this night, it means us harm.

I do not know how I know, but I do.

I shoo her back down the stairs, and we keep to the shadows when we reach the main floor. We must get out. Something is urging me to run, to flee this place. Thankfully, Annalyn is not disagreeing on leaving the abbey.

We are almost to the heavy front doors when the sound of footsteps on the staircase reaches us. We go still, and I blow out the candle providing us with what little precious light we have. Neither of us needs to speak to understand what the other is thinking. Whatever is coming down those stairs is the reason for the unease in the abbey tonight.

The smell of the hot wax tickles my nose along with the burnt scent of the smoke from blowing the candle out. Can the creature smell it? Will it know we're hidden in the shadows beside the door?

I'm too terrified to push the doors open and run. Perhaps I should, though. It might save one of us.

But is there really anything to save us from?

The clicking of shoes on the wooden floor just a few feet from us forces the air out of my lungs. I don't dare to even draw in a breath. A smell invades my senses, and I fight to keep from gagging. It's a smell I know well. I am trained in healing ways and have bandaged up my fair share of soldiers. The scent of blood is one I shall never forget, and that is what hangs heavy in the air tonight.

Maybe that is what woke me up. A smell that reminds me of fear and death.

And I have no doubt that is what this...thing promises us. Fear and death.

My grip on Sister Annalyn's hand must hurt her, but she never so much as breathes. We stand there still as statues as the creature passes by, heading toward the kitchen. Precious moments tick by as we wait to see if the thing returns, but it doesn't.

Finally letting out a breath, I push open the door, and Sister Annalyn and I slip outside. We waste no time in running. Rocks and branches cut into our bare feet as we run, but neither of us pays it any mind. Our only goal is to get away.

"The others," Sister Annalyn whispers as we run through the woods, the moon our candle now. "We can't leave them there with that...with whatever evil that was."

"We will do them no good if we go back and end up in its clutches," I tell her as we come to a stop under a tree. We are out of breath, and we need to rest for a moment. "It is better we find help and go back."

"What was it?" She looks out into the woods, better lit by the moon than abbey is at night.

"I do not know, Sister. Perhaps we will never know, but we must bring back help. Are you ready to keep moving, or do you need to rest longer?"

"I..." She breaks off when a twig snaps to our right.

I swivel my head in that direction, but I see nothing. Only the dark and the shadows cast by the moon.

"Is it out there?" Annalyn whispers,

edging closer to me.

"No. It's probably just an animal, but we should go. We have to be close to the main road that leads into the parish."

Taking her hand, we start off into the night again, careful to steer clear of the murky waters of the swamp. There are just as many dangers there as there are back at the abbey. It wouldn't do us any good to escape whatever was roaming those halls only to be eaten by alligators.

There's no running this time. We're more careful, but I keep an ear open for anything following us. I do not wish to scare Sister Annalyn, but I am afraid that thing is following us. I can't explain how I know this, but I feel it deep in my bones.

A sigh of relief escapes when I see the wide path of the road ahead. The parish of New Orleans will not be far. We can find help for our brethren there.

"We are almost there, Sister." I squeeze Annalyn's hand, but a laugh floats out into the night, and we both freeze. It wasn't a nice or gentle laugh, but a twisted one.

The creature did follow us!

"Run," I whisper and pull Sister Annalyn along with me as we try to reach the road.

Sister Annalyn's hand is ripped from mine, and I turn to see what happened, but she is...gone. There is no sign of her, and I run. I know she is lost, and the only hope I have is to reach the parish.

More laughter sounds in the night, and I push harder, finally reaching the road. I have no hope of anyone coming along. It is Christmas Eve, and most are already asleep in their beds, but if I can reach the parish, I can bang on someone's door and beg for help.

My foot catches on something, and I fall, my hands and knees catching the brunt of it. Blood seeps out of the deep gouge on my knee, and I push up quickly, knowing I can't sit here and be weak. I must move, or else I shall fall victim the same way Sister Annalyn did.

Ignoring the pain in my knees and the sting of my hands, I keep running, staying right in the middle of the road. Perhaps I should stick to the trees, but I have more fear of what is in those trees than I do of *being out in the open.*

Wind rushes through the trees, but the branches do not sway. My fear ratchets up a notch when that same maniacal laughter accompanies the strange gust of wind. What is this thing?

A few steps later, the wind surrounds me, and I turn, trying to get away from it, but as soon as I begin to run, I realize it's herding me back into the woods. I am helpless to stop it, though. There is only one path open to me, and I take it, praying with all my might that I shall not die this night.

I almost fall again when I reach the tree line, but I keep running, my legs quivering with the exertion I have put them through. I'm tired, but I can't stop. If I stop, I die. I know that. My only hope is to outrun it.

Fingers lightly graze my cheek, and I jerk away, the same stench from the abbey invading my nostrils. It's right beside me, but I dare not look. I just keep my head down and focus on not falling again.

Soon I am back at the abbey, and I

almost cry out in despair at the sight that greets me. Tears mingle with the light mist of rain that has begun. All the sisters from the abbey are hanging from the walls, their heads bent at odd angles. Sister Annalyn has joined them, her lifeless body limp. Father Dougal's head sits upon the steps leading into the abbey.

"You cannot escape me."

The voice is rough, dark like the danger of the night, but very much female. There is pain and anger in that voice.

"You and yours took my family from me, and now I shall take them back, or this will be the fate of every holy person within this putrid little colony."

The clouds clear and the moon peeks through, casting its light on the bodies swaying from the church rooftops. Their white night dresses are streaked with blood, the fabric torn, gaping bite marks all over them.

"What are you?" I whisper past the lump in my throat.

"I am something that has been here long before your kind ever walked the

Earth. I am the First of my kind, but I will not be the last."

Finally, getting the courage to look, I turn my head and study the creature. It's horrible to look upon. Its midnight skin is leathery and stretched tight over a face that is no more human than that of an animal. It smiles, and its elongated teeth are stained red with the blood of my sisters.

Hopelessness fills me. There is no escaping this thing. It is going to kill me. I only pray God lets my death be quick.

Claw-like hands reach for me, and I take a deep breath, but before I can beg for a quick death, teeth rip into the flesh of my throat and I scream, the animals in the woods surrounding us the only witness to my death.

"Mattie, wake up!"

I blink my eyes open, my hands going to my throat even as I try to calm down. I can't breathe. The dream…it was so real it had to have been a vision. One of the ghosts at the abbey.

Mary is staring at me in concern, her blue eyes dark with worry. I shake my head and sit up, pushing past her to the bathroom as bile rises in my throat. My stomach recoils at the memories of that awful dream, and hot liquid spews out of me. Mary rushes in after me, holding my hair out of my face and making clucking sounds.

When I'm done, I sit back, resting my

back against the tub. I feel empty and hollow, a deep despair that I know is left over from the nun whose death I just witnessed.

"What happened?"

"I…a vision, I think."

"Of what?"

"Remember the job I told you about? The old church?"

She nods, pulling her long blonde hair up and grabbing a scrunchie off the sink to put it up into a ponytail.

"I think I just saw one of the nuns die. Her ghost must have been there yesterday and wanted me to see what happened."

"They're invading your dreams now? I didn't think they could do that."

"There's a lot about what they can and can't do we don't know about." I take the glass of water she hands me and rinse out my mouth, spitting into the toilet. She flushes it for me. I'm drained.

"I don't like this, not one little bit." She helps me to stand and then back to the bedroom. "We need to see if there's a way to block them from doing this."

"No." I curl up on the bed and look up

at her. "They need to be able to talk to me so I can help them. Blocking them doesn't do that."

"But your dreams are haunted enough as it, Mattie. Ghosts shouldn't be allowed to add to that."

She's right about that. We both have more than enough nightmares to fill our dreams for the rest of our lives, but I can't do what she wants. I can't cut them off. They need me.

I snort at the thought.

"What's so funny?" she asked, confused.

"I was just thinking that here I am trying to keep the channels of communications between me and the ghosts open, when it was just a few years ago I did everything I could to pretend I didn't see them. Ignore them, and they'll go away. That was my mantra."

"Do you ever wish you hadn't opened yourself up and started talking to them?" She sits down, pushing my feet out of the way.

"No, because if I hadn't, you'd be dead, and I wouldn't trade your life for my peace of mind."

She smiles and rubs at her leg. I've noticed it's been bothering her a lot lately. She has a permanent limp. Zeke had all the best specialists called in to look at her injuries. They were able to alleviate some of the worst of the damage, but they couldn't completely heal her. She has scars all over her body from the knife cuts and the other instruments I don't even want to think about. Those wounds will be a reminder of what happened to her for the rest of her life, and that's something I can't take away.

"Is it hurting?"

"A little. I think it's the moisture in the air. Rain is in the forecast."

I make a face. Rain is going to make the next few days harder than it should be. We need to hunt down a primordial evil creature, and the rain is not going to be our friend.

"I see you're not packed yet." Mary changes the subject, and I let her. She hates talking about her leg.

"I figured you could do it since you're

going to dress me anyway. My jeans and t-shirts are not good enough for schmoozing Zeke's guests."

"Nope, they sure aren't. Although I'm not sure you actually own clothes meant to schmooze. I think all you have are jeans and t-shirts."

"There are a few sweaters in there too."

I'm the only person I know who'd be wrapped up in a wool sweater in the hundred-degree heat down here, but I stay so freaking cold.

"We're going shopping."

"No!" I wail. I hate shopping. "Can't you just do it for me?"

She shakes her head. "The last time I did that, you complained about what I brought back, so you're going to buck up, buttercup, and get it done!"

"You been watching John Wayne again or something?"

Mary is a closet western fan, something she tries to hide, but I've caught her watching the Encore western channel more times than I can count. She told me she and her dad used to watch them together when she was little before he died. I never make fun of her for watching for that reason alone. It's all she has left of her memories with her father.

"Maybe." She tosses me a grin and gets up, going to dig through my closet. "Do you have a dress in here?"

"Only the one you gave me when I went to Charlotte."

"You want to talk about the dream?"

I'm not startled by the sudden switch of topics. That's just Mary. Her mind runs a thousand miles a minute, and even I can't keep up with her sometimes.

"Not really. It was bad."

"Is it her ghost that's haunting the place?"

"Maybe, but it's not the ghosts we have to worry about." I tell her all about my conversation with Father David as she sorts through my clothes and starts putting things into my open suitcase. See? I knew she'd do it.

It's not until she's put the last thing into the suitcase and zips it closed that she says anything. "So you're telling me vampires are real?"

"According to Cass, vampires, werewolves, and everything else that goes bump in the night are real."

"But…" She frowns, thinking. "How are we going to get rid of a vampire? Does garlic really work? Do we need crosses and stakes? I need to do a *Buffy* binge-a-thon to get up to speed on vampire-worthy weapons."

"*Buffy*?" I ask sarcastically.

"What?"

"Mary, what you see on TV isn't real. I highly doubt this Buffy person knows how to kill a vampire."

"The show is called *Buffy the Vampire Slayer*," she says just as sarcastically. "So, yeah, I think she knows how to kill a vampire. Have you never watched it?"

"I didn't really watch a lot of TV growing up." Still don't, really. Dan and Mrs. Banks have made me watch *The Walking Dead*, but when I started making fun of it during the episodes, that stopped fast. I am not a fan. I'm the only one around, apparently. Even Zeke and Mary like it, but I just don't get it. I see enough real horror without having to watch a show based around zombies.

My eyes widen as a thought occurs. Do zombies really exist? Something else to ask Cass about.

"Oh my God!" She flings a hand over her chest. "We are so gonna binge it hard this week."

"Please, no."

"Yes!" She wags her finger at me. "You need to discover the joy of Angel and Buffy. I never got behind her and Spike. She was supposed to end up with Angel."

"Spoilers much?"

She gasps, realizing she'd just given away a good chunk of the ending. "Oh, no! I hate when people do that to me."

I sorta did that to her during *Game of Thrones*, one of the few shows I actually watch. I spoiled The Red Wedding for her.

"We're off topic. The thing we're hunting isn't a vampire, *per se*, though. It's what created vampires, according to Father David. And I got a good look at it in my dream."

Mary stays silent, waiting for me to

continue. Like Dan, she knows I'll talk when I'm ready. Pushing me for details will only make me clam up faster than Mr. Krabs and his money bags.

"It was awful. It reminded me of a leathery lizard, but it wasn't. It was like looking at your worst nightmare and then multiplying that by a thousand. It scared me, Mary."

"You don't get scared of many things. Not even the Rougarou scared you."

"That's where you're wrong, though. I'm scared all the time, but I'm really good at hiding it. World's best liar, remember?"

"Never hide that from me, sister mine. I have most of the same fears, you know. We can get through it together."

"We've gone from discussing blood demons who eviscerate people to getting all mushy and emotional over sister stuff. It's been a weird day."

"And now we get to go shopping!" She jumps up. "Go take a shower and get the puke stink off you. Then we'll go downtown and hit the shops. Before the afternoon is done, you will have clothes even Lila will approve of."

Ugh. My grandmother. I really hate feeling inadequate when it comes to her, so maybe Mary's right. Maybe showing up in some nicer clothes will help to make Lila feel a little prouder of me and me less like I'm big bright splotch of stain on a pure white backdrop.

But I do know one thing. I am not getting out of the shopping trip, so I get up, push the dream behind me, and head to the shower. I really do stink. I'll have to text Cass and tell him not to come by since Mary is dragging me downtown.

God help me get through the next few hours.

Dan ends up pulling a double at work. He's the new guy, so he gets to pick up the slack from three call-ins. He never once complained about it, but that's Dan. Mr. Dependable. Zeke got to hear me confess how worried I was. I don't want him near narcotics, but there isn't a thing I can do about it. Zeke assured me Dan can take care of himself, and I assured Zeke even Dan can't see a gun coming should his cover get blown or an itchy addict decides to start shooting for no reason.

That got through to my father. He looked as worried as I was when I finally dragged myself off to bed. Eric and Ethan were playing cards on the foot of my bed when I came in. Mary and I joined in, and the four of us played for hours. We passed out around four in the morning. Thank God I have a king-sized bed, or someone would have ended up on the floor.

I got up at five so I could I go to Dan's and cook him breakfast. Well, I'd take what Mrs. Banks cooked over and reheat it. Let's be honest, I'm not the best cook in the world. I can burn water. But Mrs. Banks promised to give me and Mary both lessons. She said I'd be whipping up restaurant-worthy meals in no time.

Riiiiggghhhhtttt.

But maybe if I can learn not to burn everything, that would do.

I take a shower and pull my hair up in a bun on top of my head. I am not in the mood for all my hair getting in my way. After I feed Dan, I need to go find Cass and fill him in on everything.

Mrs. Banks hands me the basket full of food and turns back to the stove. She's upset with me, and it bothers me. She's one of the few people in this world who means something to me.

"Mrs. B?"

"Yes, honey?"

Honey, darlin', and dear. The three terms southern people use without thought when talking to others. Lots of people up north get offended by it, but I think it's sweet. People can call me honey all day, and I'll never take offense.

Well, unless they say it in a demeaning way, but that's not the south. They don't think twice about those terms. It's just how they talk.

"I can't take you being mad at me, so can we go back to you smiling when you see me instead of this grim disapproval?"

"I'm not mad." She puts down the dishtowel she's holding and turns around to face me. "I'm scared. I know what's in that place, and the thought of you going there…very few things scare me in this world, Mattie. The creature that lives in that circle is one of them."

Mrs. B pulls out my old name, which tells me she's serious. She knows I love that name, but it's part of my past, and I want to look to the future. She rarely uses it.

"How do you know so much about it, though? I thought the locals believed what the church told them about the murders there."

"They do, for the most part, but I wasn't born in New Orleans. I was born in South Carolina. I met your father the night my husband died. There was a mass pile-up on the interstate. Tractor trailer lost control of his brakes and crashed into the cars in front of it. The ones behind it didn't have time to stop. Your father was in one of the cars, and he met me at the hospital. We started talking, and he stayed with me the whole night. Never left my side as we sat and waited on my husband's surgeon to come out and tell me everything was going to be okay. They couldn't save him, though. I was devastated, and your father took care of everything."

"I never knew that."

"Most people don't. They think I was hired from the ad he put in the paper."

"Zeke put an ad in the paper? I'd think he'd be more apt to use an agency."

"I know. His mother was shocked too, but your father isn't like most of the wealthy around these parts. He's more down to Earth."

I've noticed that about Zeke myself. It's probably why Nancy likes him so much.

"What your father didn't know is that I am part of an organization known as The Historians."

"Heather's an Historian!"

Mrs. Banks nods. "She is. We've been to a few functions together, and after I knew she was Eli's mother, we became friends."

Mind. Blown.

Mrs. Banks was an Historian.

"When your father told me about what he does and his supernatural dealings, I wasn't shocked or surprised. He was more surprised *I* wasn't shocked, and I told him who I was and who I worked for."

"Did Zeke get a little nervous?"

She smiled. "No, he told me as long as I didn't report on his comings and goings, he didn't care what I did. I've helped him more than a few times over the years."

"You've helped him steal?"

"Good Lord, no. I would never. He knows that. What I mean is when he comes across something in the supernatural world that needs to be dealt with on one of his properties, I've done some research for him."

Oh. Well, that's not so bad, then.

"When the Historians were informed I'd be moving to New Orleans, I was pulled into the South Carolina office and told all about the blood demon and the circle of power trapping it. It was the single most dangerous thing in and around the city. That's not to say other things aren't dangerous, but this thing is kept half-starved, only feeding on those foolish enough to wander past the wards. That thing is more than dangerous because of its hunger, Mattie. If you go there and prod the beast, it won't just bite, it'll kill you."

I can hear the fear in her voice, see it on her face. But now that I know what's there and that it's killing people, I can't let it stay there. It should have been dealt with long ago.

"I know you're afraid, but what about all the people who will die if I don't do something, Mrs. B? Kasey will hire crews, the protection ward will be broken when the ground is broken, and that thing will be free. People will die. Innocent babies. It eats babies. Did you forget about that part? How can you expect me to just sit on the sidelines knowing what's going to happen?"

She flinches at that last part. It's true, though. Historians only gather information. They never actually act on the information. That's wrong. I won't say it to her, but it's a truth I feel wholeheartedly. If you are armed with information, you have a duty to protect those who can't protect themselves.

"I'm going to do what I can to take it down. Cass will help. We may need to involve all the hunters in New Orleans and call in even more backup, but that thing is going down."

"You don't understand what it is."

"But I do. God made darkness, and then he created the light to chase the darkness away. That thing said it was here before the humans were, and I think it was made when the darkness was made."

"How do you know that, and what do you mean it said that to you?"

"I had a vision yesterday. Of the night the nuns died. I saw everything through the eyes of a young nun. I think her ghost wanted me to see what I was up against, and she showed me in my dreams. I've seen its face, heard its voice. I know it probably better than anyone alive, Mrs. B. I can take it down. Don't doubt that. It takes more than some dark creature to destroy me."

Mrs. Banks starts muttering something in a language I don't understand. She speaks several languages, and now I know why. She's an Historian.

Again…mind blown.

"I'm going back there, Mrs. B, but if you really want to help to keep me safe, find me all the research you can on that thing. I need to be armed with information. Heather said she'd email me what she had, but I'm betting you know more than she does. Can you do that for me?"

She still looks troubled, but she nods. "You are as stubborn as your father."

"I'll take that as a compliment." I hug her and head to my car, careful to tuck the basket in the seat so nothing spills. I'm tempted to put the seat belt around it, but it would look pretty crazy driving around downtown with a picnic basket strapped in.

After shooting Cass a quick text to let him know I'm swinging by his place later, I get in the car and head to Dan's.

He lives about three miles from the police station. Zeke helped him find the place, and Dan never said a word about the discounted rent that my father managed to secure him. Mostly I think because he knows he'd never be able to afford the building, and it really is close to work. He can walk if he has to.

Dan's building is a nice one, with a doorman and everything. I nod to him as I lug my picnic basket with me. I'm on the approved list of people who have access to the building, and I've been here enough that he knows me by sight.

"Thanks," I say when he opens the door.

"Need a hand with that?"

"No, I got it, but thanks."

He goes back to people watching, and I head to the elevators. I really, really hate elevators. If it wasn't for the very heavy basket of food, I'd have taken the stairs, but Dan lives on the sixth floor, and no way am I hauling this up six flights of stairs.

When it finally dings and I'm able to get out, I breathe a sigh of relief. Ever since the hospital morgue fiasco, I don't do elevators if I don't have to. I still haven't been to the basement of this place, and I have no plans on it anytime soon either. Doesn't mean a ghost has the same idea, though.

I let myself in and turn on the lights. He hasn't gotten home yet. Good. It'll give me the chance to set the small table and warm up the food. Once I have everything in the oven and set to the temperature Mrs. B told me, I take out the plates and silverware to set the table.

I'm in the middle of pulling glasses out of the cabinet when I hear the key in the lock.

He doesn't notice me right away, so it gives me a chance to study him. Dan looks tired and in need of a good night's sleep. I'm worried about him. I'm not sure he's sleeping much, and given his line of work, he needs sleep.

The second he senses me, his face clears and breaks out into the biggest grin. It's like all the tiredness flees from his expression, and he tosses his keys into the bowl on the small table next to the door.

"Hey, baby." He comes into the kitchen and wraps me up in his arms, his mouth coming down on mine for a good morning kiss. Like always, it's not that hot flash of heat, but a slow burn that starts in my belly and fans out into flames that consume every inch of me.

When Eli kissed me, it was this instant hot flash, but this? This burns deeper and brighter than anything I've ever experienced. It's why I know I would have always ended up with Dan, but the one good thing that came out of Eli's death is it allowed us to escape the pain I know having to choose would have put the brothers through.

"You're an early morning surprise," he says when he pulls away.

"I thought you'd be hungry, so I have breakfast."

"Take out?"

"Pfft, no. I cooked."

He arches a brow, and I laugh. "Well, Mrs. B. cooked, and I have it reheating in the oven."

"That's my girl." He nuzzles my neck. "Let me shower, and then we'll eat, okay?"

"Want some company?"

That lazy grin I love appears. "Sure, baby. Cut the stove off, though. Don't want to set off the fire alarms again."

He's never going to let me live that down, is he? Right after he moved in, I attempted to make popcorn in a pot. He says it's the best way. Only I let the oil get too hot, and it started to smoke out the kitchen, setting off the sprinklers and the fire alarm in the building.

Make one mistake…

"You know I love you despite your lack of culinary skills, don't you?"

"I do." I cut the stove off as asked. "Now come show me how much you love me."

Dan laughs and pulls me toward his bedroom. The morning is looking up, and it's barely daylight.

I leave him sound asleep with a note saying I'll be back later. I have things to do, specifically camera-y things. Which requires Ethan's help, so I make the drive back to my dad's and roust Eric, Mary, and Ethan. None of them are too pleased since we sat up so late last night, but hunting waits for no man. Or woman.

"Where did you get these?" Ethan asks as he plunders through the thousands of dollars of special cameras.

"My dad had them designed for us. They'll actually capture a ghost on screen."

"We've captured ghosts before."

Mary and I both roll our eyes. "No,

Ethan, you haven't. You've captured anomalies like the blurring of light or spots of sunlight, a lightbulb, or flash reflecting off a camera lens. There is nothing a ghost hunter has today that actually captures images of ghosts."

Eric tosses him our version of an EVP detector and EMF reader all built into one. "Now, this is designed to not only record ghost voices, but it'll show you if there was a disturbance in the electromagnetic field at the same time. That's how you know it's real. Ghost energy disrupts the EMP, so no disruption, no voice."

My phone buzzes, and I look to see a text from Cass. Shoot. I forgot I told him I was coming by. Dan distracted me. Quickly, I send him a text asking him to meet us at the church. It's time to get to work.

"What makes your equipment better than ours, though?" Ethan turns on the voice box, as Eric calls it, and waves it around. It statics a little when it hits Mary and more so when he aims it at Eric, but with me? It's like a nuclear bomb going off. I am nothing but ghost energy, and that poor box doesn't know how to deal with me.

Ethan points it toward himself, and it goes quiet, but he swings it back in my direction. His eyes just about bug out of his head as he shuts it off and stares.

"Told you, Ethan, I'm a reaper. I'm made up of ghost energy."

"Wow," he whispers and gently sets the box down. "I...wow."

"You'll get used to her." Eric slaps him on the back. "Help me load this stuff up in the van."

"But the cameras...why would they record a ghost image when you don't think ours do?"

"Because they're spelled."

"Say what?"

"Spelled." There is no hiding the smirk on Mary's face. "The cameras have a spell engraved into them that allows the lenses to see and record a ghost. These cameras record in night vision, thermal vision, and spectral plane vision all at once."

"That...what?"

"Ethan, there's a lot more to us than even you know, but you're going to learn it all if you hang around and come work for us."

"Work for you?"

"Eric, why don't you explain it to him while you guys load up the cameras? Mary and I will bring out the microphones."

"Sure thing, Hathaway."

"Think he'll run screaming?" Mary picks up one of the heavy duffels and starts toward the door, glancing down the hallway where Zeke's office door is firmly shut.

He's pissed at us because we wouldn't agree to stay away from the church. Kasey refused to outright sell to my father. I knew he wouldn't, though. He was proving something to his own father.

"I don't think so. He's too enamored of the supernatural."

Mary snorts. "That'll change *real* quick." She stops at the door. "Why did you tell him about all this, about you?"

"Because he's always hanging out with us now, and I think if he and Eric ever quit dancing around each other, he's going to be our new brother. But if they're never anything more than friends, he's still going to be around because he's Eric's best friend. He'll see things that can't be explained, and it's better he hears it from us now rather than later."

She nods and goes outside. I grab the other duffel and follow her to the state-of-the-art van Zeke had designed specifically for us. It's a prototype model, and if it works out, we'll have more made. This thing is nicer than even Doc's. It comes equipped with super comfy pull-down cots for sleeping too. Take that, Scooby Gang.

My nose scrunches up at the thought of The Ghost Chasers. I hope we can talk Ethan into joining us. Wade is eventually going to come across a real ghost or demonic spirit and get them all killed. I've come to know Ethan, and I don't just like him, I'm starting to care about him. He's important to Eric, so he's important to me. I swear if Wade gets him killed, I will beat that boy to within an inch of his life and make him wish he was never born. And that's a promise.

Smiling, I toss the duffel in the back. I'm worlds away from the old me, and she'd probably punch me in the face for going soft. Letting people get close, letting myself care…she would have run far and wide to escape that.

But I like this me. She's a good person with the same edge the old me had, only I think this version of me is better. I'm still trying to shake the last remnants of the Rougarou curse and all the old fears and insecurities it brought raging back to life, but it's getting easier every day.

Eric snaps his fingers in front of my face. "Earth to Hathaway."

I blink. "Sorry, I was just thinking."

"About what?" He wags his eyebrows up and down. "You had the softest smile on your face. Thinking about your morning with Danny Boy?"

A blush rushes to my cheeks, and I duck my head. Leave it to Eric to baldly throw that out there where everyone can hear it.

"No, I was not, thank you very much."

"Really?" He crosses his arms and

leans against the van.

"Really." I shut the back doors. "I was thinking about how the old me would punch me right in the face if she could see me now."

He laughs. "She wouldn't just punch you, sugar, she'd stomp you so far into the ground, you'd never dig yourself out of the hole."

He knows me better than even Mary does.

"Why's that?" Ethan asks as he and Mary finish the checklist we made up for equipment and things. Wouldn't do to leave something behind. Those cameras cost ten grand each. I nearly hyperventilated when I saw the bill. That didn't even include the cost of the spells to ensure they worked the way we wanted them to either.

Yes, I still break out in hives over the mere mention of money, but I knew I couldn't skimp out when it came to the equipment.

"You never knew her when she was in foster care." Eric shoves off the van and goes up front to the driver's side. "Let's get going. I don't want Cass there by himself."

Neither do I. While that thing may sleep during the day, I don't know enough about it yet to understand its weaknesses. Neither Heather nor Mrs. B have gotten me the information I requested yet. I sure hope they do sooner rather than later. Wouldn't do to try to tackle it without knowing more than I do now. Been there, done that with Deleriel. I sure as heck don't want to ever do it again.

It takes about an hour to reach the church, and Cass is already there along with Robert. Caryle has a few more days of school until Christmas break, for which I'm grateful. I don't want her near this place.

"*Chèr*." Cass nods toward Eric and Ethan but hugs me and Mary. "How are my beauties?"

Mary laughs at his not-so-subtle wink in her direction. She thinks he's the most charming guy around, but she has no girly butterflies in the stomach around him, so she says he's firmly in the friend zone.

"Hey, Robert." I toss a smile in his direction. "You remember Ethan?"

He grunts. Robert's version of yes.

"He's going to be working with us on this. He knows more about cameras than anyone I know. He'll be teaching Eric, and Mary is going to handle the audio and computers from the van. I'm hoping Robert will keep her company since he knows computers. I don't want any of us by ourselves."

"It's just ghosts, *chèr*." While Cass's accent isn't absent, it's not thick either. He's been around Ethan enough to be familiar with him, but he's still a little guarded.

"But it's not just ghosts. There's more to the property than we knew. Do you guys know what a primordial evil is?"

Robert's eyes widen so much, they might as well have jumped out of his head and done a jig on the ground.

"Who tol' you dat?" Cass's nostrils flare, and his gaze sweeps over the woods surrounding us. He and Robert have both gone on high alert.

"Father David. He had no idea the church sold this property. Some overeager accountant marked it for auction without checking the codes or something."

The cousins start cursing in French. I know enough of the language to know exactly what they're saying.

"Do I need to set up a swear jar?" I put my hands on my hips and glare at them. "We are on church grounds, and there is no cussing in or around a church."

"Yes, ma'am." Robert's unable to hide his smile.

"Cass Michael Willow, you had better agree to no more cussing, or I promise you, you are gonna meet Mattie Louise Hathaway."

Cass smirks. "No offense, Emma, but I'm bigger and stronger than you are. I think I'd win in a fight."

Eric nearly bends over laughing at that little comment. "Dude, Mattie'll take you down. She fights dirty, and I'd bet on her any day of the week. I taught her how to fight myself when she was little, and she's only gotten better. Girl's been taking kickboxing classes with me."

I notice the odd look Ethan gives him, but Eric doesn't. It's something he'll have to explain to Ethan at some point, but that's his story to tell and not mine.

"I don't think so."

Before the words are even out of Cass's mouth, I move and sweep his leg out from under him, and he falls. My knee lands in the middle of his back, and I have his arm twisted up behind his back at a very painful angle. When he tries to buck me off, I pull harder.

"Still think you can handle Mattie Hathaway?" I whisper. "She's not Emma Crane. I keep her buried, but all that anger and fear she lived with is still inside, and it can bring her back to the surface whenever I need to. I like the new me better, but I'm not afraid to be the old me either."

"She's awesome," Ethan says, affection in his voice. "Think Dan will beat the crap out of me for having a crush on his girl?"

"Dude, I'll beat the crap out of you. She's my sister."

Ethan shrugs and grins unashamedly. He's cray-cray.

I let Cass up, and he sweeps the dirt off his pants and a long-sleeved black t-shirt.

"I would say dat was luck, but I have a feelin' it wasn't."

"It wasn't."

"Good to know, *chèr*, good to know." There's a grudging respect in his eyes that wasn't there before. Now maybe he'll believe me when I say I can take care of myself.

Against anything but a gun, my inner voice taunts.

That'll be moot after this weekend, I remind said voice. Knives used to be my biggest fear, but guns are now side by side with that fear.

"Tell us everything while we unload all dis stuff." Robert opens the van doors and lets out a whistle. "Dis is nicer den Doc's ghost hunter van." The Willows have adopted my nickname for Doctor Olivet.

"He'll be totes jealous," Mary agrees.

"Totes?" Cass arches a brow.

"Totally," Mary explains and reaches

for the first of the cameras. "I'd think having a sixteen-year-old sister would keep you up to date on all the slang."

"Caryle knows we'd torture her until she stopped saying it. It's a ridiculous word."

"Says you." Mary sticks her tongue out and grabs another camera. "Ethan, Eric, let's get this inside so Em can fill the boys in on our blood demon."

"Blood demon?" Cass pales. "Did I hear dat righ'? She said blood demon?"

"Unfortunately, yes." I wave them to sit down on one of the van's cots and take a seat myself to tell them everything I've learned. It takes a while. By the time I'm done, all the equipment has been unloaded, and Mary is talking to Eric and Ethan up near the church doors. The boys and I join them.

"Dis we did not know," Robert says. "We need more help."

"Father David said they were going to call in the hunter who put the original protection spell in place to make sure it's still standing. I'm not sure if Kasey broke ground anywhere on the property or not.

It's over twenty acres."

"*Merde*," Cass spits out.

"Hand over a dollar." I hold my hand out.

"For wha'?"

"Cussing. Zeke is teaching me French, so don't think for a second I don't know what that word means."

Robert laughs, which earns him the stank eye from Cass, but the boy dutifully pulls out his wallet and hands me a dollar. I stuff it in my pocket until I can find a jar to turn into a swear jar.

"You just tryin' to take all my money, *chèr*."

I stick my tongue out at him and then go inside the church. This time I don't have to hide what I can do and let my reaping abilities out in full force as soon as I step over the threshold.

Letting myself slip beneath the surface of the icy cold lake I imagine my abilities sleeping in, I find them quickly and push to the surface. Every time I dive beneath the waters of that lake, it feels like I'm drowning. I'll never get past the fear of drowning, thanks to the ghost who did drown me, but it's almost easy now. Zeke helped me learn to deal with it since he's a reaper too.

As soon as I reach out, I feel them. I must have really had my abilities locked down when we walked the place with Simon. They're all rushing at me, demanding to be heard, to be helped. If not for the tattoo Caleb gave me, I would have been overwhelmed. Thanks to that nifty little ink, my sanity and my mind are safe from them. And I'm able to sort the voices, only listening to one at a time.

The nuns are all here, trapped by the brutality of their deaths. The creature isn't keeping them here. They're here to protect those who accidentally wander onto the property. They feel it's their duty. I don't think I can convince them to leave as long as the creature still remains here. They've been here for over a hundred years doing what they can to protect the innocent, and they won't give that up just because I tell them I'm going to fix this. They'll believe it when they see it.

It's not just the nuns, though. There are

others here as well. Not all of them good, not all of them innocent. Some were very bad people in life and remain bad people in death. We need to stay away from those. I will deal with them after we deal with the blood demon, but no one goes anywhere alone. These ghosts are malevolent.

"What do we have?" Cass is following close behind, leaving the others to set up a base of operations in the front room.

I blink, realizing I've found my way into the kitchen area of the old church. I need to work on paying attention to my surroundings. Ghosts may not be able to sneak up on me when I'm in the zone, but all manner of other creatures can. I'll talk to Zeke about maybe arranging some training sessions to help me out.

"Lots and lots of ghosts. More than I counted on, and some of them not very nice. We need to be careful. No one goes anywhere alone. I mean that, Cass, not even you and me."

"*Oui, chèr*, I agree. I doan like dis place any more den you do."

"Come one, I need to go upstairs."

Not that I want to, but I have to. Taking the steps one at a time, I climb the spiral staircase. With every step, I feel the heaviness of the dark memories these walls hold press in on me. It's like walking through quicksand and fighting to breathe as the air thins.

Cass knows not to touch me, but he's so close, all I have to do is lean back, and I would press right up against him. I take comfort in that. He's not Dan, but he does make me feel safe, despite getting me into more trouble most days than even I can get myself into.

The darkness is so thick up here, it chokes me, and I gag on it. I wave Cass away when he tries to help. There's nothing he can do as images from that night assault me.

I give in to the vision and let myself get lost in it, knowing Cass is here to pull me back if I need him to.

The wide, arched windows have no glass, allowing the cold December winds to reach inside and caress the people lined up around the walls of the circular landing. The bedroom doors are open, the rumpled beds within visible in the moonlight.

Droplets of blood catch the rays of the moon as they drip off the creature's long, claw-like hands. It's in the middle of the circle of nuns, who stand motionless, unable to move. It's not fear that keeps them still, but true paralysis. I can hear their thoughts somehow. They were told to be still, to not move or speak.

And that's what they're doing.

None of us can move.

Us…it's then I realize I'm inside one of the nuns, watching through her eyes. It's why I can understand the order given to hold still. It was said in Latin, maybe, but I understood it perfectly.

The tattoo I have prevents me from feeling physically what happens, but emotionally, I feel everything.

And right now, all I can feel is a deep, soul-wounding fear.

"Did you think you could get away with what you did to my brethren? To my children? Did you think you would not pay for what was done to us?"

None of us understands what she's referring to. Her children? We did nothing to her children. We would sooner hurt ourselves than hurt a child.

I know it's female, because it's a mother's anger we face. She may not look human, but she's very much a woman. A monster who is a mother. What could be more deadly?

She stops in front of me, and the stench is horrific. She smells of death; the rot of decay mingles with the coppery scent of fresh blood. My eyes sweep to my fallen sister lying on the ground, her flesh ripped where the creature tore into her. Her eyes are glassing, staring at nothing. She died unable to scream, unable to move.

The creature's hand comes up, and one of her fingers slides up and down my cheek. She leans in closer and sniffs.

"Such purity I smell in your soul, my child. You would do well as one of us."

One of them? No. I will not.

She chuckles. "You think you have a choice?"

There is always a choice between good and evil. I will always choose my Lord's path.

"Your Lord," she spits out. "You have faith in Him, do you not, child?"

She can read the thoughts in my mind?

"Yes, I can."

Dear Lord, deliver us from this evil.

She laughs. "Your Lord will not be saving you this night. You think He cares what happens to you all? Why has He not intervened? Why has He not sent his archangels down to destroy me for defiling his holy temple? Because you are nothing to him. But you *are* something to me. You are a message. Give me my family, or your brethren will keep dying."

She moves so quickly, I don't have time to even think before her teeth tear into the flesh of my shoulder. Silently, I scream as she continues to bite chunks of my flesh, the blood seeping from the wounds staining my white nightdress.

I can't even fall because she told me not to move. I stand there while she slaughters me and scream inside my head.

When she's done, she doesn't move away. Instead, she holds out her arm and uses one of the razor-sharp fingernails to open the flesh in her inner arm.

"Drink, child." She puts the wound against my mouth, and I automatically do as she says, following her orders even as I say *no* over and over in my head. There is no use, though. Her blood fills my mouth, slides down my throat, and when she thinks I've had enough, she pulls away and helps me to sit down.

The pain begins almost immediately. It

splinters through me like a shard of glass breaking into thousands of tiny pieces after a fall. I can hear the blood pumping in my veins, feel the sickness spread from my stomach outward, consuming everything in its path.

It hurts.

That's all I am for the next few minutes, one big mass of pain as I feel the filth eat away everything good inside of me, leaving its stain behind as my body slowly dies.

And all through this, I watch the creature continue to slaughter my brethren. But as the minutes pass, I find myself less and less inclined to feel horror or anger toward this thing. Instead, a burn begins in my belly. Not the same as when the tainted blood first hit it, but just as painful. My throat is dry and raw from thirst. I can't bear it.

"Almost time, my child. Just a minute more, and you will be mine."

The creature is kneeling beside me, stroking my hair. Her face is the one I see when the strangest thing happens. One minute I'm curled up on the floor in more pain than any mortal should ever have to withstand, and the in the next minute I'm standing, looking down upon myself and the creature.

What is this new sorcery?

"There you are, my sweet girl," the creature croons. She beckons one of the remaining sisters to her. Sister Lara. She's only a year older than me. The girl comes as she's bid. I see the absolute terror on her face, but her feet carry her forward, and she remains silent as we were bid to do.

The creature pulls the girl down to my body.

I'm looking at her with this expression of need and hunger, and my eyes have brightened. The green is so vibrant it reminds me of home, of the hills of Ireland. There is no memory of home in those eyes, though. They are not me anymore. I see only the darkness that lives in the creature's eyes in my own.

And that's when I know. My body died, and all that remains is the evil that entered it. She cast me out and replaced my soul with her own darkness.

That is not me.

I try hard to believe it when I see myself reach up and painfully pull Sister Lara to me, watch as I sink my teeth into her arm and drink from her. I toss her aside, able to stand now and move to the next of our sisters. One by one, the rest fall at my hands.

Except for Mother Superior. As the sisters fall, she ties a bedsheet around their necks.

I feel them surround me and look up. They're all here, watching alongside me as we all die. Mother Superior is the last one standing. She ties a bedsheet around her own neck.

The creature smiles at her. She does not drink from the Mother. Instead, she snaps her neck and turns to the shell that was my body.

"Come, child, help me with these husks. Then I'll take you to rest. I have an errand I must run, but I can do that on my own. You must rest while your body acclimates to its new state of existence."

I watch as the two of them drag the sisters out the window. We move cautiously toward them, but they can't see us. Or at least I don't think they can. In truth, Sister Lara passes through me without so much as a flinch on her way to pull Sister Alice outside.

We can see what they are doing. All of the poor sisters are being hung along the rooftops, left out on display in their nightdresses for all to see. It is shameful what this creature has done, and on Christmas, no less.

A golden light opens up behind us, and we turn. For all the horror we have witnessed tonight, there is nothing but love in that light. It's beautiful, and we step forward.

"No, my sisters, we cannot enter the light."

The voice of our Mother Superior stops us, and we glance toward her.

"She was not wrong when she said God let this happen. But for a reason. We must protect the innocent. We must stop them from entering this place, these grounds. Our duty now is to them."

As much as I want to go into that light, I cannot. Mother Superior's words ring true. Perhaps our Lord did not forsake us but put us on this path to save others. We cannot ignore that.

The light begins to fade, and we all watch as it disappears.

Mother Superior is right. We were not forsaken. We were meant to die this night so that we may protect others in the future.

And that is what we will do for as long as this creature lives.

Cass catches me before I fall.

"Emma, are you okay, *chèr*?" He sounds worried. God only knows what I look like. If it's as bad as I feel, he has every right to be worried.

"I'm good." I clear my throat, but I can't seem to get rid of this insane thirst. It's left over from the vision, the bloodlust the sister experienced when I was in her body. It's carried over to my physical body. That shouldn't be. I'm not supposed to experience what they experience. Silas promised me.

"Let's get back downstairs." Cass places an arm around my waist and half carries me back downstairs. I sense his unease, but more than that, I can sense something else.

When I first met Cass, I thought he was as human as they come. Now that all my abilities are waking up, I know he's not fully human. I can smell it on him. Which is totally weird, but it is what it is. I can also feel that he's different. It's the strangest thing, but it's like cuddling up to a warm fuzzy blanket and discovering those little lint balls that make it irritating. Cass has little lint balls tucked all over him. I'm not sure yet what he is, but once I figure it out, he and I are gonna have a chat.

I don't think even he realizes he's not quite human. He hates supernatural monsters, so I don't think he's going to take hearing he might be one very well.

But that's a problem for another day.

"What happened?" Eric demands when we walk into the main room. He rushes over and takes me from Cass, helping me to sit down in one of the chairs they unloaded from the van. Granted, it's just a fold-up metal chair, but my shaky legs are more than grateful for it.

"She had a vision, I t'ink." Cass rummages around in the cooler sitting by the computer table. It's not ours, so I assume he and Robert brought it along. He produces a bottle of water, for which I am eternally grateful. I drink the whole bottle down and he hands me another. This one I take a little slower.

"Whoa, there, Poseidon." Eric pulls the bottle away from me. "Slow down or you're gonna be sick."

"I'm thirsty." I reach for the bottle, and he hands it off to Mary.

"Nope. I refuse to clean up puke, and we all know you and Mary puke harder at the sight of puke, so I'll be the one stuck doing it."

"He's right." Ethan nods. "I love you girls, but not enough to clean up your puke. That's all you, buddy." He slaps Eric on the back.

"Wha' did you see?" Robert steps closer. "Is it why you're so thirsty?"

"Yeah."

That gets all their attention.

"What did you see, Hathaway?"

"Remember I told you about my vision

yesterday?" When they nod, I continue. "That nun never saw what happened upstairs. She ran before she could. I saw what that thing did to them through the eyes of the nun who became one of her new children. When her body died, her soul was cast out. She's here, and she showed me what we needed to fear. The thirst overcame her before she died, and it's lingering in my psyche."

"It's making more monsters." The grimness of Robert's tone matches the awful feeling in my gut.

"And t'ings just got dat much more dangerous."

"I thought you were protected from a ghost making you feel things?" Mary comes and squats beside me, concerned. "Is the tattoo not working anymore?"

"I don't know."

"You need to talk to Silas."

I nod. "I will. But not until we get this place wired from top to bottom. We need a better idea of what we're dealing with. Eric, will you call Father David and see if he can tell us where the protection circle starts? We'll need the van outside that circle."

"Who's staying in the house?" Ethan asks.

"No one." I look around at the computers they've already set up. "It can't know what we're doing. I want all the big cameras gone. Use the smaller ones we can attach to the ceilings or high on a wall."

"Emma…"

"No." I cut Cass off. "You didn't see what I saw. You'd be saying the same thing if you did. I've always trusted you, Cass. It's your turn to trust me."

He doesn't look too happy, but he agrees. "I'm goin' to call in some backup, dou. We be needin' all de help we can get."

"Agreed. We need reinforcements. Now, let's get this done, so we can set up a stakeout."

None of them argue with me after that. It takes us a good three hours to wire the church with the cameras, the microphones, and the motion sensors. Those, we put outside. They couldn't be hidden in the bare confines of the building, but we could hide them outside in the ground.

"Now what?" Ethan wipes the sweat from his brow.

"Now we go to Mama Luigi's and pig out on pizza." I'm still starving, and this thirst won't let up. "Then we come back here and wait in the van."

"How far out from de church will de computers pick up de cameras?"

"Five miles," I tell Cass. Even I had been shocked, but when you're dealing with spelled equipment, it works far better than your stand pieces do.

He whistles. "Da…"

My glare cuts off the curse word about to fall out of his lips. Cass grew up in the bayou, and he was around cussing all his life. He knows I don't use it, and normally, I don't mind when others do. But this is a church, and I won't budge on this.

"Come on, Bruiser, let's go before Cass ends up owing you a small fortune." Ethan swings an arm over my shoulder and starts leading more toward the door.

Robert is still standing in the middle of

the room, hands on his hips, with an expression of worry.

"What is it?" I ask him.

"Our scent will be all over dis place. They'll know we were here. And it's been here for a century. Who knows how many more it made?"

"We can't mask our scent, Rob. We can only control what we can control and deal with the rest later. Let's go eat, and then we can come back and worry about our scent."

He sighs but finally starts to follow us out the door. I don't miss the way his eyes sweep the woods and surrounding area. That starts a nagging thought in the back of my mind, but it'll keep until we get settled in at the Italian restaurant we've all come to love. We found it while scoping out the food places close to Tulane. We could walk to Mama Luigi's from our campus in less than five minutes. They don't do delivery, so Mary, Eric, and I have hoofed it on more than one occasion for a pizza to die for.

Mama Luigi's is not your typical Italian restaurant. It doesn't cater to the fancy date night dinners. Instead, it caters to the college campus. The tables are newer and the chairs comfy. They also have big farm tables in the back for bigger groups like ours. The walls are a relaxing cream color with photos of New Orleans and Tulane's campus. The staff are wearing jeans and a green Mama's t-shirt. I love this place.

None of the bigger tables are available, however, and we end up shoving three tables together. The staff here knows us, so they don't bat an eye. We order six large pizzas. I know it sounds like a lot, but with four grown boys at our table, five of those pizzas are history. Well, truthfully, maybe all. Mary and I will probably end up with salad and cheese sticks unless we grab food like a man who's been on a deserted island for a year.

Once the drinks are delivered, Mary leans forward and stares the Willows down. "Tell us about vampires and what we need to know."

"You t'ink de rules of vampires apply to a primordial evil?"

"No, Cass, but I think they apply to the children it made."

"She's right. We need to give dem a crash course." I notice Robert's accent is a little thicker today. He must really be upset.

"So give us the scoop." Her eyes are shining brighter than I've seen them in a long time. I think it goes back to this whole Buffy thing and how she fangirled about it.

"Vampires are not what you see on TV or read in books," Robert explains. "Well, most books. Dey aren't all sparkly and romantic. Dey're clever, dangerous, and hard to kill. De only real weaknesses dey have is sunlight and fire. Sunlight will cause severe burns all over dere bodies, and fire is the only real way to kill a vampire. You take de head, and den you burn them both in separate fires."

"Garlic and a stake to the heart don't do anything?" Eric asks, frowning. He and I are both monster movie fans. We've probably seen every one ever made, including the old ones from the fifties. In my opinion, those are some of the best because they relied on storytelling and not special effects.

Robert laughs. "Boy, you threaten a vamp with garlic, dey'll use it to season you right before you become lunch."

"That sounds…uncomfortable." The face Ethan makes has us all laughing.

"Now, a stake to de heart," Cass takes up the explanation, "it's an urban legend. Stakes won't kill a vampire even if you pierce dere hearts. It won't paralyze dem either. Wha' it will do is piss dem off to de point you will die slowly and painfully."

"Silver hurts dem." Robert arches a brow when I drink down my own Coke and reach for Eric's. "We have silver bullets and arrows dipped in silver. I need to go home and stock up. Any of you know how to shoot a gun?"

A full body shudder ripples through me at the mention of the word *gun*. I hate them.

"I know you have issues wit' guns, Emma, but you need to learn to use dem. Dey are one of our best weapons against de supernatural when equipped with silver." Robert never blinks when he tells me this.

"I know…I just…" I shake my head and slump down in my seat. I know he's right, but that doesn't make this any easier. "Maybe we can set up a training schedule for us all?"

Cass smiles, knowing how hard this is for me, but I can see the pride in his eyes.

"Good girl. Rob and I will handle de weapons for dis job, but you all need to get up to speed sooner ra'der den later, *oui*?"

"So how do you take one down, then?" Mary frowns.

"You shoot dem full of silver to slow dem down. Silver won't kill dem, but it hurts dem. Once d'ere weak enough, you can take de head."

"Is there anything that can paralyze them?" I'm curious about this. I'd rather paralyze them than attempt to shoot a vampire. "I'm assuming they're fast?"

Robert snorts. "Fast ain't de right word, *chèr*. Inhuman speed, unparalleled vision and hearing. Dey are de perfect predator."

"And the blood demon?"

"A primordial evil only has one weakness—de light. No'tin else hurts dem. And even light won't kill dem," Cass says. "I'm not sure how to take one down. We've never faced one before."

"Know anyone who has?"

He shakes his head.

"Well, fudgepops."

"I'll make some calls, get some help down here. We won't go inside tonight. We'll study our enemy from afar." Robert's smile appears, and I see why. Cindy, the waitress I know he has a crush on, delivers our food, along with two people carrying varying dishes. "Hello, Cindy."

She gives him a flirty smile. "Long time, no see, Robbie."

Robbie?

Cass chuckles. I'd like to see anyone but this girl call Robert Willow "Robbie." He hates nicknames.

"Been busy, *chèr*." He leans back, tilting his chair on two legs.

"Too busy for me?" she drawls.

"Never too busy for you, darlin'."

Ohh, boy's got some game.

"Then you'd best call me or I'm gonna go find someone else to take me to the movies this weekend." She plants his plate down in front of him a little harder than necessary. Not that it bothers Robert. The twinkle of devilment in his eyes deepens.

He pulls her down and whispers something in her ear none of us can hear, but we sure can see the blush on her face.

"Okay," she whispers and walks away a little unsteadily.

Like I said, boy's got some game.

"Care to share what you told Miss Cindy?" Cass grins.

"Nope." Robert reaches for a whole pizza. "Dis be mine."

All the boys start grabbing trays. See? Mary and I shake our heads and reach for the cheese bread and the bowls of meat sauce. Getting a slice of pizza around these boys is impossible.

My phone buzzes, and I groan when Zeke's ringtone comes on. He's pissed at me, but I know if I don't answer, he'll come looking for me since he knows where I was. He's worried.

"Hey, Papa."

"Everything go all right at the church?"

"It did. We got it wired up without any hiccups, and now we're pigging out on pizza and cheese bread."

He lets out a sigh of relief. "You're not going inside tonight?"

"No. We want a better understanding of what's going on, so we'll be staying outside in the van well beyond the protection circle."

"About that. I spoke with Father David. The circle extends one mile in every direction around the church. I thought you might need to know that."

"Cass was going to call him, but thank you for doing it, Papa."

He clears his throat. "Yes, well, your safety is always my top priority. You know that, Emma Rose."

"I do, Papa."

"Well, the reason I'm calling is a package arrived for you. It's rather large."

"A package? I wasn't expecting anything."

"It's from your brother."

"Nathaniel?"

"I would hazard a guess that it's your Christmas present. I do hope you remembered to get him something as well?" Zeke's manners are kicking in. While he despises the fact my brother is a member of the Dubois family, who are eviler than the Cranes, he respects that Nathaniel is my brother. He hasn't forbidden me not to see him, but he lets it be known he dislikes him.

"Of course, I did. I put it out in the mail a few days ago."

"I'll put it in your room. Mrs. Banks asked me to have you all come for dinner. She's found some information she wants to share with you about the thing that's inhabiting the church."

"It's not actually in the church, Papa."

"You know what I mean Emma Rose."

I snicker at his irritation. He knows I do my best to be irritating.

"We'll swing by for dinner. Cass and Robert will be there too."

"We will?" Robert asks, his mouth full. I shoot him a disgusted look. Gross.

"We'll see you for dinner, Papa."

"See you soon, *ma petite.*"

At least he stopped calling me Emma Rose. He does that when he's extremely furious with me or when he's scared to death. I think both situations apply here.

Once he hangs up, I text Nathaniel. My brother and I text daily. If I forget, he calls to make sure I haven't gotten myself into trouble. His grandparents are a little upset with him at the moment too. He decided to move down here to ensure I didn't end up dead or worse, as he put it. It meant leaving an Ivy League school for a more mundane law school without all the prestige attached to it.

The Dubois are more than pissed. He played it down, but I'd heard his grandmother screeching at him one day when we were Skyping, and she called his cell. I am not their favorite person because they blame me for his decision.

Granddaughter of the year, I will never be to either of my grandmothers.

"I have a thought." Eric follows his statement with a very loud belch.

"Gross." Mary shoves him away from

her and into Ethan. "You deal with his nastiness."

Ethan laughs and belches himself.

"Disgusting." Mary slides her chair farther away from them. "Stay over there and be gross together."

The boys bump fists and down another slice of pizza.

"What thought did you have?" It's hard not to laugh at the three of them.

"Sunlight hurts them, right?"

Robert nods.

"Can we create something to simulate the sun's rays that we can hit them with?"

"Even if that were possible, we couldn't get it any time soon."

"We need R&D at the new headquarters." Eric's expression is serious. "And a witch we can trust to do all our spellwork for us at a monthly salary rate. I saw the bill for the cameras. Even I nearly passed out when I saw the number."

"You really are serious about dis, aren't you?" Cass asks, a look of speculation in his eyes.

"Yes. I plan on making sure hunters

across the US have everything they need to stay safe."

"It won't be easy to get dem to trust you."

"Nothing worthwhile is ever easy."

"God's truth, dat." Cass clinks his glass against mine.

"Well, let's finish eating and then head over to Zeke's. Mrs. B has some information for us."

Information I hope we can use to our advantage or will at least keep us from dying.

Thankfully, I'm not driving when Nathaniel rings. Mary is. The boys are in the van, and the Willows said they'd meet us at Zeke's for dinner. They needed to finish their Christmas shopping while they were in town.

"Hey."

"Did your package arrive yet?" Nathaniel yawns into the phone.

"Did you just wake up?"

"Maybe. Did your stuff arrive?"

"Uh, I think so. Zeke called and said I had a package from you."

"You're not home, though?"

"Nope. Mary and I are getting some last-minute things for our stakeout tonight."

"What kind of stakeout?" I hear him get out of bed and start walking around.

"Nathaniel Buchard, you best not be thinking of going to the bathroom while I'm on the phone with you."

"Would I do that, darlin'?"

"Yes, you would."

He laughs. "You're right, I would, but not today. Now, tell me about your stakeout."

"The Foundation got hired to de-ghost a building. We already set up all the cameras and other things, but we need snacks to make it through, so we're headed to the grocery store."

"That makes no sense, Emma. You don't need surveillance on ghosts. You can deal with that by yourself. I've seen you take on a soul eater and survive. A random haunting shouldn't be that hard."

"Well, we thought it was just ghosts, but turns out the land is inhabited by what's called a primordial evil. A blood demon, specifically."

He's so quiet I think the call dropped and actually pull it away from my ear to look down. Nope, still connected.

"Nathaniel?"

Mary glances at me then back to the road.

"Nathaniel, you still there?"

"I'm here." I hear a door shut. Well, actually, slam would be more accurate. "I'm trying to calm down before I say something I'll regret."

"I know how dangerous it is."

"Do you?" he hisses. "Because if you did, you wouldn't get within a thousand miles of that thing."

Great, now he's pissed at me too.

"I'm not marching in there with no plan. We're doing recon. The thing is behind a protection circle."

"You think that matters?" Another loud noise echoes in the phone. "It's the type of demon that create vampires. It can get in your mind even behind a protection circle and bring you inside. No one is safe from it. All you're going to do is get yourself, Mary, Eric, and whoever else is stupid enough to get near it after dark killed."

Well. I hadn't thought of the mind

control as being exempt from a protection circle. That's a problem.

"It has your scent, Emma." Weariness tinges his voice. "Once it gets dark, it'll track you and whoever else was there. If you're anywhere near it, it'll reel you in. Don't go near it. I think I have something that will help, but I need to go home and look through the vault."

"Vault?"

"Yes, vault. I think we have something to help repel the mind control."

"Is it black magic?" He knows how I feel about that.

"Yes, it's black magic, but it'll protect you."

"Nathaniel…"

"Don't Nathaniel me, Emma Crane. For once in your life, listen to your big brother whose only goal is to protect you. Please don't go there tonight. I'm trying to get a flight to Georgia now. Just wait until tomorrow."

A plan is already forming, and promising him I won't go near there until tomorrow will keep me from lying.

"I promise I won't go near there until

tomorrow."

He lets out a breath. "Thank you."

Now I feel bad. While I didn't technically lie, I let him believe what he wants to believe, and that makes me a horrible person. But he's right about one thing. I'm not letting anyone near that thing if it can get into their heads. I know how that feels since I'd just relived it. I won't bring my family to a place where they have to stand and silently watch as we all die, unable to move or help each other.

Not doing it.

"Okay. I'll be there as soon as I can." He hangs up without even giving me a second to respond.

"He just hung up on me."

Mary shrugs. "Boy has no manners."

"We're not going anywhere near there tonight. We'll monitor the cameras from here."

"I thought we had to be within five miles of them."

"To watch live, that's true. But I have it set to upload to a cloud service that's got so much security, the CIA would have problems accessing it. It's set to upload every couple hours. We'll be able to watch the footage after dark around eight or nine tonight. At least the first of it, anyway."

"Think we'll ever just come across a simple haunting?"

"God, I hope so. These ancient evils are starting to wear me down."

"Hashtag truth, girl." Mary nods and pulls into the driveway leading up to Zeke's plantation. "What did he say to change your mind?"

"The thing can reach out beyond the protection circle and use mind control and force us inside the circle."

"You're serious?"

I nod. "The vision I had earlier, I was reliving everything the nun did. I couldn't move, couldn't speak, couldn't defend myself. I have no doubt if that thing gets into our heads, we'll die. I won't put anyone in that kind of danger."

Except for myself.

But if I die, so does Dan.

How am I going to do this without killing him?

"I need to talk to Silas. You go on in. Zeke will have a fit if I summon Silas inside his house."

"*Fit* doesn't describe the word." Mary opens the car door and gets out. "I'll tell him you're talking to someone so he doesn't come outside."

"Thanks, Mary."

I wait until she's inside before I call for him. When a few minutes pass and he doesn't appear, I start internally shouting his name over and over.

"What?" he gripes when he finally materializes in the driver's seat. He's wearing his normal black dress pants and white button-up shirt. His hair is a little longer than last I saw him, and there's blood streaked across his face, drops of it marring the pristine whiteness of the shirt.

"Well, hello to you too."

"I was in the middle of something, my darling girl."

"Sorry I interrupted whatever you were doing, but this is important, Silas."

I think the seriousness of my voice finally breaks through his irritation.

"What happened?"

I tell him about the vision and the aftereffects. "I thought the tattoo was supposed to stop that."

"It is."

And in the next second, we're standing in his studio. I forget how quickly he can do that. It normally takes me a few minutes, but I guess centuries of practice gives him an edge on inter-dimensional plane travel.

"Take your shirt off. I need to check that tattoo."

For once, I don't argue. I have on a tank top underneath, and the tattoo on my shoulder is visible with it still on. Otherwise, we'd have had an argument. Grandfather or not, I'm not stripping in front of anyone except for my boyfriend.

His finger traces the design of the tattoo, and he starts muttering.

"What?"

"I have to fix this. I missed it when we repaired your tattoos after the Rougarou attack." He walks over to the small closet off to the side of the room where he has his spelled ink. "On the table."

Instead of going to the metal table where he puts his soul-sucking victims, I opt for the wooden one where he sits and draws and has his morning coffee. It's not as big as the other table, and my feet hang off, but I am not getting on that metal gurney by choice.

"It's probably good that you did," I tell him when he comes back out carrying a bottle of ink and his tattoo gun. "It allowed me to understand the true dangers of thing I'm facing tonight."

"What thing?" He loads the tattoo gun with the ink and pushes the strap of my tank out of the way.

"What do you know about blood demons?"

"Where did you come across one of those?"

"The Hathaway Foundation got hired to de-ghost an old church, and we discovered it was inhabited by a primordial evil. The place was sold by mistake to the public. The church tried to buy it back, but the owner isn't selling."

"The Red Church?"

I let out a little hiss when the needle

hits my skin.

"Yes."

"Do you understand what lives there, Emma Rose?"

"I do. That's why having this tattoo go screwy helped me. I was able to understand that it can control you in a way nothing else can."

"That thing is something even I won't go near."

And that's saying something. Silas has been around some pretty evil things, including the Fallen Angel Deleriel that I defeated.

"Well, unfortunately, I can't leave it there. The new owner will bring in more people if I don't do something."

"And you're afraid those people will die?"

"Not just that. If they break the ground and disrupt the protection circle, it'll get out along with all the vampires it made."

He doesn't say anything else while he repairs my tattoo, which is concerning. Silas only ever goes quiet when he's angry. Granted, he doesn't like to talk during these tattoos, but I can feel the anger vibrating off him. He may not be showing it, but I can definitely feel it.

"What's your plan of attack?" He puts the tattoo gun down, and I turn to look up at him. Yup, there's rage burning in his eyes.

"I, uh, don't really have one. I was gonna wing it."

"Wing it." His fists clench. "How many times have I told you, my darling girl, I am the only demon who is allowed to hurt you? And even then, I hate it, but I will to get my point across."

Memories of him peeling the skin from my face rush up. It's something I'll never forget or forgive. Silas and I have a rocky relationship. We understand each other, though.

"Do you even know how many vampires it's created?"

"No."

His nostrils flare. "Of course not. You're going to rush in there and get yourself killed."

"That's not the plan."

"You just said you didn't have one."

"Not getting killed is always the plan."

He snorts.

"Well, I was hoping you could help me. Do you know of anything that can keep it out of my head?"

"Keeping it out of your head is not the problem. It's faster than you, stronger, and has no qualms about killing to feed. And the only weakness it has is sunlight."

"That, I already know."

"And yet you are insisting on making this thing your problem?"

"I can't let innocent people die when I could do something to stop it."

"You and your need to save the world, Mattie Louise Hathaway. It's going to get you killed."

He almost never uses that name. He's beyond pissed.

"And I'm not about to let you do that."

Before I can blink, his hand is on my head, and that's the last thing I remember.

Something wet wakes me up. I scrunch up my nose and turn away, but it only follows. My face is being assaulted by a very eager wet tongue. Peaches.

"Easy, girl, I'm up." I laugh when the whole bed shakes with her bounce. When my Hellhound wants attention, she gets it one way or another. Dan can attest to that. The hound has been known to knock him over and sit on him until he gives in and agrees to play with her.

Why is Peaches in my room, though? I haven't gone and gotten her from Silas…

Silas.

Looking around, I realize I'm in my room at his home. He knocked me out to keep me from going back to The Red Church. Well, he's got another thing coming if he thinks he's getting away with this.

I get up and try the door. It's locked, but I expected nothing less. Time to leave, though. I know how to open the portal from here back to my plane. Closing my eyes, I remember exactly where I was when I left and imagine a doorway opening.

Only it doesn't. What did Silas do?

I pound on the door. "Silas! Open this door right now and let me go home!"

Nothing.

He's either ignoring me or he's gone back to whatever awful thing he was doing when I interrupted him.

Either way, I'm stuck. He's obviously put up some kind of ward to keep me here. There has to be a way around it, though.

Peaches pushes her head up under my hand, and I pet her absently. He put her in here to keep me company, most likely, or he knew I wouldn't have a meltdown around her. She keeps me calm, for some reason.

"Okay, girl. There has to be a way out of here."

Think, Mattie, think.

Despite the situation, I laugh. Even though I insist everyone call me Emma, I guess deep down I still think of myself as Mattie Hathaway. And that's not a bad thing. She's who made me who I am today, and I'm proud of that person. I'm proud of Mattie Louise Hathaway.

Peaches goes over to the closet door and butts her head against it. Several times. Do I have treats in there for her or something?

"What are you being nosy about?" I open the door, but it's completely empty. I didn't think I had any clothes here, but I can never be sure. I've spent a lot of time here the last few months.

Peaches whines and shuts the door with her head.

"Peaches?" I lay my hand on her head to try to keep her from hurting herself, but the second I do, something weird happens. A strange electrical shock travels up my arm, and the hound shimmers. Actually shimmers. She butts the door again. This time when I open it, I'm looking at my car sitting in front of my father's home.

"Did you do this?" I ask her, and she whines. She steps through the doorway and walks over to my car.

Well. That solved that problem. As soon as I step through onto the paved driveway, I look back, sure I'll see my room, but it's gone.

Okay. That just happened.

"Come on, girl. Let's get inside before Silas realizes we're gone."

The minute I step inside and call out, the room is flooded. Mary and Zeke come running out of the office.

"Where have you been?" Mary demands.

"Uh, I was with Silas…"

"He said you came back," Zeke spits out right before he hugs me so tight, I can't breathe. "I was terrified you were gone again."

"No, he just decided to keep me safe in his own fashion by locking me in my room. If I couldn't get out, I couldn't go back to the church."

"Did he hurt you?" Zeke demands.

"Papa, I'm fine."

"I'm going to kill him."

"For what? For doing what you wanted to do?" I shake my head. "Silas is a lot of things, but when it comes to keeping me safe, he'd go to the same extremes you would. You can't fault him for that, Papa."

"Why do you always defend him?"

"I honestly don't know."

"Because she loves me."

Silas is leaning against the doorframe, and Zeke growls. Papa has demon proofed this house six ways to Sunday, but Silas always finds a way to get in.

"Oddly, I do, and I'm still not sure I'm okay with that." I mean, he did tear a strip of flesh from my face, and I've been around enough messed up relationships to know I shouldn't love the demon who did that, but deep down, I think he hated himself for doing it.

"I'm perfectly okay with that." His British accent is almost gone. Strange.

"Of course, you are." I roll my eyes

and move away from Zeke. "But you can't lock me in a room and forbid me to do something any more than Papa can just because you're worried."

"You were talking about going up against a primordial evil, my darling girl. These are creatures that came into existence even before demons. I don't know how to take one down."

"For once, Silas and I are in agreement. I don't want you anywhere near that thing."

"Papa, Silas, I can't let it be. What happens when a construction crew comes in and breaks the ground and the protection circle that holds those things inside disappears? What then? Do you think I'll be able to live with myself knowing I could have prevented it?"

"But you won't be preventing it if you're dead, now will you?" Silas's anger starts coming through, and his accent thickens. "What happens then, Mattie? Do you think your father will survive losing you all over again? And Daniel? He dies if you do."

"Then I won't die."

His face morphs and twists, something sliding beneath his skin, and I wonder what he really looks like. Is the demon under the disguise of a human? I should be disgusted, but I'm not. Maybe being around Silas has helped me to accept my own demonic blood just a little.

"Take a chill pill." Eric slides between me and Silas. He's the only person who knows what Silas did to me. I think he hates Silas a little for it, but like me, he also knows Silas did that to make sure I was in the frame of mind to be able to take on Deleriel and survive. And I almost didn't.

"Boy, I will slice you to ribbons..."

"No, you won't," I interrupt him. "Eric is my brother, and you will not harm a hair on his head, or you'll deal with me."

"You..." He goes to reach for me, and Eric and I both take a step backward.

"Calm down, Silas." He's in a mood. I haven't seen him like this since the days leading up to Deleriel.

"Calm down?" He advances, and I back up until my back hits a wall. "You want me to calm down when you're standing here talking about going up against something so old and so evil, there isn't a living being on this Earth that knows how to come close to even stunning it, and you want me to calm down?"

Zeke tries to rush us, but he stops, frozen. I look down at his feet, encased in ice with streams of a black substance climbing up his legs. I know that; I've been trapped in it myself. The first night I met Silas. He did that to me.

"Silas, stop. Don't hurt him."

"Him? Don't hurt him? What about me, my darling girl? I'm the one who's watched over you since you were born, the one who walked the floors with you when you were sick, and your mother was so high she couldn't remember her own name. I'm the one who...what do you think losing you will do to me? I can put as many protections as I can on you, but in the end, it's your choice to do the things you do. Free will." He spits on the floor. "The worst mistake ever made was giving you all free will."

"You did all that?"

"How do you think there was always food in the house when you were little? Your mother? She was too high. She found out I was coming to see you, and she blocked me. That's when I lost track of you. She did something so I couldn't find you. That's why it took me years to locate you. Or you would have been safe. That, I promise. You were never supposed to be in foster care or with someone who cared more about her next fix than you."

"I don't remember any of it."

"She did something. I don't know what. I've been trying to figure that out since the day I finally found you."

Why don't I remember?

"I taught you to draw. You had a natural ability, and you and I would sit for hours and color. That's one thing you didn't forget."

"Did you know what I could do? Is that why you…"

"No. You were too young. I just wanted to make you happy and safe. You belong to me as much as you do Ezekiel, Mattie Louise Hathaway."

And that's when it hits me. He's just as terrified for me as Zeke. Maybe even more so because Zeke at least didn't try to stop me by force. I knew Silas loved me, but I never realized how much. He loves me the same way my father does.

And I don't remember any of why he loves me like that.

"Mama took those memories?"

"She was afraid of me. She thought I was going to hurt you. Her sister told her I was going to ruin you, to harm you like Ezekiel wanted to."

"She was high. She would have believed anything."

"Your mother was a good person, Mattie. She loved you despite her addiction. Sometimes that addiction got in the way of caring for you, and that's when I stepped in. She tried to kill you to keep you safe. Not because she wanted you dead, but it was the only way she knew to protect you in that particular state of mind."

"I know that. It took me years to understand it. How old was I when you lost track of me?"

"Two weeks from your fifth birthday."

"I wish I could remember."

"There was something done to you, something I think your mother allowed, but it wasn't to keep you safe."

"Rhea said that too."

"They did something, and I'm still trying to determine what, exactly, but it removed every single protection you were born with. As soon as I met you that night, I knew something was wrong. It's why I was so hard on you, why I pushed you so much, why I…" He breaks off and takes a deep breath. "You had to be ready or you wouldn't survive. You were supposed to be a means to an end, but out of all of them, you were the only one I took care of, the only one who meant a thing to me. I didn't know if you had the abilities I hoped you did when I squirreled you away from Georgina, but it didn't matter to me. You were you."

He tucks a stray strand of hair behind my ear, and his finger traces the path of the strip of skin he took from me. "I'm sorry, but I had to. You had to be afraid of me so I could prepare you."

"I know that."

"You hate me for it, though."

"Sometimes."

His nostrils flare, and his eyes turn darker.

"But I forgave you, Silas, because I understand why you did it. Realizing why Mama did what she did, it helped me understand you. You both did very bad things to protect me."

"You forgive me?"

"Yes, *Grandpère*, I forgive you."

I've only seen Silas cry once before, and that's when he picked me up off the ground in Deleriel's lair, whispering to me not to die, that he wasn't going to let me die. Ordering me around as usual, but with tears streaming down his face. I don't remember a lot of that day after smashing my and Deleriel's soul, but I remember that.

"But that doesn't mean you can lock me away every time you think I'm about to do something stupid. Or freeze Papa so you can have your say. Unfreeze him, please?"

I catch sight of Ethan's expression. If

this weren't so serious, I'd fall over laughing. The poor guy sure stepped into it.

Zeke stumbles as soon as he's free, since he was moving forward. Eric catches him before he falls.

"How dare you…"

I wave Papa's anger away. "What's done is done. I know you both want to keep me away from the church, but you can't. What you *can* do is help me. Silas, you said you had something to keep them out of my head?"

"What are you talking about?" Mary asks.

"Mind control. They can apparently get in our heads, even outside the protection circle and force us to walk past it. An easy meal."

"I didn't think of that," she says. "I really need to binge *Buffy*."

Silas rolls his eyes, something he's picked up from me. "Buffy would die if she ever faced a real vampire."

"Bite your tongue. Buffy is awesome."

"Don't argue with her. It won't end well." Eric glances at Ethan. "You good?"

He nods slowly. "I think so."

I notice Zeke shove his hands into his pockets. He walks over to Silas and says something I can't hear. Silas nods.

I am a little dazed over Silas's confession, but I can't let that get in the way of what I need to do.

"I know what you're planning, and it won't work." Silas points his finger at me, the black nails sharp. "Going in there alone or with that reaper won't ensure your safety. You need numbers to take down a nest."

"What's a nest?"

"She doesn't watch a lot of *Supernatural* either. Only when Cass comes over and forces her to." Mary looks around. "I think maybe the dining room would be a better place to talk things over, and Cass should be here."

"I'll call him," Eric volunteers and pushes Ethan out ahead of him.

"Boy." Silas stops him with a hand to his shoulder, and I tense, prepared to defend him. "Does that one belong to you?"

Eric glances at Ethan. "He does."

"Will he be a problem?"

"No."

"Make sure of it, or I will. Do we understand each other?"

"We do."

"What was that all about?" Ethan whispers as he goes by me.

"I'll explain who Silas is later. For now, just don't piss him off."

I'm not sure there is any explaining away Silas, but I follow them all out of the room and toward the dining room.

Now, to figure a way of salvaging my plan.

Cass, Robert, and four other hunters I don't know arrive a few hours later and we all sit down at the dining room table. It's made to seat thirty easily. Mrs. Banks prepared a full spread to feed everyone.

I check my watch for the hundredth time. It's after nine. Zeke brought in the flat screen he keeps in his office. It's a forty-two-inch television, big enough for everyone to see the first of the footage. Robert is working on his laptop so he can bring up all the camera screens at once. I'm not sure that's the best way because we might miss something, but he gave me the look when I mentioned it. The look that says, "Do you know computers?" I left him alone after that.

Ethan and Eric are both on laptops too, going through some of the footage and audio files. All I can think about is how to get out of here undetected, but Silas hasn't taken his eyes off me. Not once. He knows me too well.

I can't put them in danger, though. I can't.

"You worry too much, *chèr*." Cass sits down beside me. "No'tin gonna happen to anyone. I promise."

"He's right, my darling girl." A briefcase appears on the table in front of us. He opens it and inside is a glass bottle full of dark red liquid. At first, I think it's black, but when the light catches it, it's definitely red. "This will keep them out of your thoughts, and should you get bitten, this will also paralyze any of the demon's children. It won't do much against the blood demon, but it'll take down the vampires momentarily. Enough time to take their heads."

"What is it?"

"Dead man's blood doctored with a particular herb only grown in the fourth circle of Hell."

"Things grow in Hell?" Cass asks. He's not exactly comfortable with Silas, but he's stopped wanting to stab him with his blessed blade every time he sees him. That's progress, in my opinion.

"Only very bad things." Silas grins and picks up the bottle. One of those little plastic cups like you see attached to NyQuil bottles is produced as well. He unstops the bottle and pours a healthy dose into the cup and hands it to me. "Bottoms up, my darling girl."

"You want me to swallow a capful of blood?"

"Dead man's blood, but yes."

"No."

"Why not."

"Not only is it just gross, it's against the Bible."

"Pardon?"

"Do not drink the blood, for the blood is the life," Cass says. "Well, that's the shorter version of Leviticus, seventeen thirteen."

"Exactly."

"And in this case, it's the only way to

save your life." Silas pushes the cap toward me. "Drink it."

I shake my head stubbornly. "I won't drink blood."

"Yes, you will." Nathaniel strides into the room, looking as arrogant as always. "I see you managed to find what I was stealing from my grandparent's vault."

"Nathaniel." Silas nods toward him. "Where do you think I got this?"

"You can't get in there."

Silas only smiles and closes the briefcase. There's a large D emblazoned on the cover. Nathaniel blinks several times but then dismisses it. I'm sure he'll inform his grandparents they need better demon-proofing on the vault.

"The demon is right, though. This is the only thing to protect you. It's not going to stop them from slicing and dicing, but if one of them sinks their teeth into you, they'll go down in about three-point-five seconds."

"I won't do it."

"It's a religious thing," Cass tells him. "She may not talk about her religion, but she's devout."

Nathaniel's lips thin. "God will forgive you."

"I know he'll forgive me. That's not the point."

"It's very much *the point*," Nathaniel argues, his hazel eyes blazing. "I did not come all this way and steal from my grandparents, only to have you throw a stubborn, mule-headed fit!"

"I am not..."

"Yes, darlin', you are. You want to be a hunter, then start acting like a hunter. None of the men in this room would blink at swallowing this if it meant taking down a nest of vampires."

"What did you get us into, Cass?" one of the men I don't know demands. "First you involve us with Cranes, then demons, and now a Dubois?"

"This is The Hathaway Foundation now, boys. We're here to help." Mary smiles at them, and the youngest of the group blushes. She has that effect on men. She bats those baby blues, tosses her blonde hair over her shoulder, and they're putty. "You'll need these to communicate." She starts handing out earpieces. "Microphone and headset in one. No pressing of any buttons needed. As soon as it's on, you'll be in constant communication with each other."

"Vampires can't hear them either," Zeke adds. "We had that in mind when they were made."

The oldest of the three—Brett, I think his name is—begrudgingly takes the small earpiece.

"Targets in view," Robert calls out. Cass shakes his head and hands me an iPad. The same view on the big screen is also on the iPad. Another gift from my father.

Cass and I watch as three women enter the room. They're dressed in jeans and t-shirts. Dark-haired, but pale. Even in the light of the moon, I can see how pale they are. They turn in a circle, eyeing the room. I zoom in on their faces and notice their nostrils flare wide, sniffing.

"They caught our scent, didn't they?"

"Dat dey did, *chèr*, dat dey did."

More filter into the room, acting more like cats hunkered down than anything human.

APRYL BAKER

"They're faster than we are," Cass says, "their instincts more animal than human."

"They remind me of a cat." I lean forward, fascinated. They move with a grace I'm sure even a cat would be jealous of.

"It's not far off. They stalk their prey, play with it when they catch it, and then eat it. Vampires are vicious, just like cats."

"You don't like cats?"

"Never met one who liked me."

An idea takes root, and I grin. Cass rightfully looks alarmed.

"How many you counted so far?" Brett asks.

"Eleven." Robert looks about as happy as I am right now. "I'm not sure we have the numbers to do this. That big of a nest is no joke."

"We have dead man's blood. They won't be draining us dry tonight." Cass stands and takes the bottle of blood and the small cap. He drinks the dose that's already poured out and then passes it around.

I watch, completely grossed out, as all the hunters drink it down. They really expect me to drink it too. Mary grimaces but takes hers like a man. Ethan shakes his head and gets stared down until he too drinks. Eric shrugs and chugs his down. Nathaniel is next, and then it's my turn.

"Bottoms up, buttercup." Eric pours it himself and hands it to me. "You either drink it willingly, or they'll hold you down while I pour it in your mouth and cut off your air supply."

"You wouldn't dare."

"There's a lot of things I've dared for you, Hathaway. You can do this one thing for me."

"I hate you."

"I love you too."

I take the capful of dark liquid, screw up my face, and swallow like a good girl, all the while apologizing to the man upstairs. I hope he forgives me for this, but I know it's to protect me so I can protect others. Maybe that'll wash out the sin.

"Good girl." Silas grins like a proud papa, which I guess he is. He acted like a father when I was little, even if I can't remember it. He's not lying. Silas is a lot of things, but a liar isn't one of them. I trust him and what he says to me more than I do Zeke, even.

"Here, you'll need these as well." Mary starts handing out glasses that are fitted to wrap around your head. "They have three different fields of vision. One is thermal, one is electromagnetic, and one is night vision. You can adjust what you need from these tiny little buttons on this side." She shows off the pair in her hands. "Go ahead, put them on."

"This is military grade," Brett says, a little awe in his voice. "How did you get something like this?"

"I assure you, not even the military has anything like this." Mary flashes him a grin. "This, gentlemen, is strictly developed for The Hathaway Foundation. When you work with us, you get the best equipment, from guns to specialized voice recorders. And you get paid."

"Paid?"

"Yes, Tyler, you get paid." Mary winks at the boy.

"That's what The Hathaway Foundation offers. A regular paycheck, help when you need it, and the equipment to not get yourselves killed."

Well, Mary is going to be officially in charge of recruiting and the go-between for the Foundation and the hunters. I don't have the people skills she does.

"Regular paychecks?" Brett looks between Mary and me.

"Taxes withheld and all," Mary says. "You'll be regular tax-paying citizens with a job, just like everybody else. Only you'll get really cool toys and the backup you sorely need. We're setting up a school too for those of you who have children with no mothers or fathers at home to watch out for them while you're away. Dorms will be provided. This is at no cost to any of you. Should a child be left an orphan due to the job, we'll take care of them. This foundation is to make sure you come home alive and if you don't, then you know your family will be taken care of."

"Why should we trust a Crane who has a demon grinning at her like she's the best thing this side of the Mississippi?"

"Because I didn't grow up a Crane. I grew up as Mattie Hathaway in the foster care system. I only found Zeke a couple years ago. I'm not some rich kid who thinks she's entitled to everything. I grew up so poor, I had to steal food to eat. I know what it's like to be hungry, to fight off attackers in the form of foster parents, and I've survived two serial killers. Trust me, I don't have the manners or the class of someone born into a wealthy family. I'm just me. I'm a survivor, and I want to help all of you survive too. That's why you should trust me."

"We can leave dat for later. Now, we need to get to de church and set up. We know dey be at least eleven and a blood demon. No one's ever taken one down, but we sure be about to try tonight." Cass looks at us. "Stay safe."

And there goes any chance of me doing this by myself. They're all going to be in danger.

"Mary, you and Robert are in the van monitoring the cameras." This, I won't budge on. The girl has a limp, and she can't run as fast as we can. "Nathaniel, you and Cass are with me. Boys, you're together. I don't want anyone alone at any point."

"You running the show, little lady?" the youngest drawls. Texas, I think.

"Yes, sugar, I sure am. Get in line or get out." I didn't' want him here anyway. The more people, the riskier it is, in my opinion. Granted, I've never gone up against a vampire, but I've done some stealth work. Big numbers are always a minus, not a plus.

"Yes, ma'am." He mock tips his hat at me.

"Then let's gear up and head out." Cass nods and leaves the room, his hunter friends following.

"Uh, guys, why are we doing this tonight?" Ethan asks. "I thought the plan was to do surveillance tonight and come up with a plan? Preferably one where we attack during daylight hours? When they're sleeping and less likely to murder us all?"

"We don't know where dey hide during de day," Robert explains as he packs up his laptop. "It's more dangerous at night, but dey have our scents. Dey will be out looking for us, and it'll be our best chance at clearing the nest."

"And they can mentally track you," Mrs. Banks says as she comes into the room. "It's what I wanted to tell you. I looked through all my research, and that's what makes them the most dangerous. Each person has a unique scent, a flavor, if you will. Inside that scent is a trace amount of your soul energy. They can latch onto that and find you in your dreams. They can make you come to them. Letting them live while they know what you smell like is more dangerous than attacking them at night on their home turf."

"They can really do that?" Ethan finally starts to look worried. Thank God that boy is coming out of the "OMG, I'm a hunter now" look. This is dangerous, and he needs to respect that. Not fanboy.

"Not all of them, but the blood demon can. I spoke with Heather Malone earlier, and we pooled our resources. Father David didn't hold anything back from you. We know of their tracking ability because we have studied them from the moment we knew of their existence."

"Don't you think it's something the Historians should have told the Church?" I ask. Really. Maybe the Historians were just as bad as the Church.

"I do, but it's not my place to say. I watch and record. It's up to the Elders to determine what is shared."

I want to snort, but instead I thank her. She found out important information and at least shared it with us. I know she loves me, and that's why she broke the rules of her order. I have to remember that and not lump her in with the stupidity of that decision to not share.

"Is there anything else we should know?"

Mrs. Banks looks directly at me. "Don't get killed."

"Not planning on it. Silas?"

"I'll be there."

"Keep an eye on Mary, will you?"

"I'm not an invalid." Mary stands and puts her hands on her hips. "I can take care of myself."

"But you are my sister, and I'm not getting you killed on my watch after everything I went through to bring you home."

That haunted look flickers through her eyes, and I note that Nathaniel stiffens at my side. He doesn't know anything about Mary and Deleriel or what I actually did to defeat a Fallen Angel, only that I did.

"Yes, ma'am." She gives me a watery smile and files out the door after the others.

"Hey, how did you get here so fast? I thought you were still at law school?"

Nathaniel shakes his head. "No. I got home yesterday. It's not a long flight from Georgia to New Orleans."

"I'm glad you're here." I may not fully trust him yet, but he's my brother, and I feel better with him at my side. I don't question my feelings. One day he may decide to kill me, but for now, he's here to help, and that's what matters.

"Ready?" Nathaniel asks and offers me his arm like the gentlemen he was raised to be.

There's only one thing left to do since

my plan went out the proverbial window. I link my arm through Nathaniel's and follow my family outside to the van and hope I don't get them all killed tonight.

The mist is out in full force when we roll up one mile outside the protection circle. The van will stay here, and we'll hoof it the rest of the way. No flashlights. We don't want to give them that advantage, but I'm not sure it matters. They have super sniffers. Better than even shifters, according to Cass. They'll smell us long before they see any flashlights.

At least the sky is clear and there's a full moon.

"You bring the flamethrowers, Brett?"

"Right here." He hauls out three of the biggest pieces of equipment I've ever seen. "Ever use one of these?" he asks me.

"I don't think I could carry one of those. They look heavy."

"We can adapt them to a smaller, more lightweight version you can handle, Hathaway."

Eric is studying the flamethrower like it's his new Transformer on Christmas when he was a kid. Did they have Transformer toys back in ninety-four? I'll have to ask him about that.

"Wha' do we have?" Cass is leaning into the back of the van, checking the monitors.

"D'ere not dere. I don't see dem anywhere at the moment." Robert's gaze is glued to the screens, while Mary is putting on headphones to listen to the audio. We have mics in places we couldn't easily put cameras. She's scanning through all the audio loops. It's her one job tonight. Be our ears while we can't.

"Brett's gonna take point on dis, *chèr*. He's cleared more nests den anyone I know. You cool wit' dat?"

I nod. If he can keep people from

getting killed, then so be it. I've come to terms with the fact I can't keep Eric and Mary away from this any more than Silas and Zeke can force me to sit out. It wasn't an easy realization.

"When they come, they're gonna come fast and hard." Brett pops his trunk and starts handing out guns. "These are equipped with silver bullets. You get a shot, take it. It might slow them down enough to keep you alive."

I shake my head when he passes one my way. "I don't know how to use a gun."

"Then take this." He pulls a long-bladed knife out of the trunk, and I shrink away from it. Without thought, I shove my hands in my pockets. They're shaking. I've had some really bad experiences with knives. We don't mesh well.

"No, no knives."

"You need a weapon."

"Trust me, I have a weapon." Being part demon and part god, I have more than a few things at my disposal.

He doesn't question me, just hands a

gun to Nathaniel. When he slides the chamber and checks the clip, it's all I can do not to jump out of my skin. Dan's near-death experience with a gun is something that will haunt me for the rest of my life.

"Eric, Ethan, you're on guard duty with Silas. He's here, but I don't know where."

"Will do boss," Eric says.

"Let's move." Cass motions for me and Nathaniel to follow him. We turn our earpieces on and break off into two teams of three. Cass, Nathaniel, and I head toward the back of the church while the other three take the front.

Nerves eat away at me as I slink through the night, hugging the wall of the church. Cass is in front, with Nathaniel behind me. We make our way slowly to the back of the church where a heavy wooden door is firmly closed.

"Stay close," Cass whispers.

I turn on my night vision and look toward the trees and the creepy fog. I see nothing out there except the emptiness of the woods and the swamp beyond the woods. My vision is tinted green, but I'm good with that. Mary, Eric, and I wore these things for weeks getting used to them.

The Loa are here as well. I feel them all around, pushing me back, but I can't give them what they want. I have to go inside. People are counting on me. Innocent people who aren't even aware of the danger. I have to save them if I can, even if I don't know who they are.

"What is that?" Nathaniel whispers.

"What?"

"You don't feel it?"

Cass and I turn our heads to look at him. "You feel the Loa?"

Nathaniel's eyes widen. "The Loa are here?"

"*Oui.*" Cass head turns in all directions. "They want us to leave."

"We can't, though." Nathaniel's fist clenches. "I want to leave, but we can't."

And that sums up how all three of us feel.

I hear the door creak open, and Cass motions for us to go in. He brings up the rear, with me in the lead, Nathaniel close on my heels.

As soon as I'm inside, I let my reaping out. The ghosts are everywhere and willing to help. That's what they decided to stay for, to help, and I'm their best bet at getting rid of this thing.

Where are they?

Thank God I don't have to speak out loud to talk to ghosts.

Everywhere.

Specifically, where?

Get down, they shout at me.

"Down!" I scream and duck, Cass and Nathaniel not hesitating in following the order.

Something flies past us, a streak so fast, I barely see it.

Up, run!

"Get up, run."

Nathaniel pulls me to my feet, and we take off running.

Cass doesn't move, and I falter looking back. He's still on his stomach, gun clutched in his hand, eyes closed. He's waiting. Waiting for it to come for us. I won't leave him.

"No," Nathaniel hisses, trying to force

me to go.

"He's my family as much as you are, and I'm not leaving him here. They're too fast."

Shots ring out from the front of the church where the other team is. I run back toward Cass, and then something grabs me, slinging me against a wall. When I slam into it, all the breath leaves my body, yet Cass hasn't moved. He's biding his time.

Nathaniel, however, has dropped to a knee, his back against the wall, and is firing the gun at something I can't see. I switch to thermal and look for the cold spots, mentally shooing the ghosts out of the room so I can see what my target is. Once the ghosts are gone, there are three cold spots left—one on the ceiling, one to the left of Nathaniel, and one right by Cass's head.

He has to smell it. I can smell the stink of death on it from over here.

More shots ring out, this time from Nathaniel's gun. The cold spot next to Nathaniel goes down, and he's on her with a wicked-looking blade. Her head comes rolling toward us.

A keening sound starts low in the room, then spreads out.

They're mourning.

And they're pissed. The one by Cass lashes out, and that awful darkness that lives in me rises, pouring strength into my limbs, and I stand, walking toward Cass and the creature. It leans over him, and he fires two rounds right into his neck. The thing growls, and I can smell the burnt flesh. The silver burns much the same as a fire does.

He goes for his blessed blade, but the other one that Nathaniel wounded is on him, its claws tearing into him. The one leaning over, clutching at its throat, is my target. More shots fire off. I'm not sure if it's Cass or Nathaniel, but my focus is on the long red hair.

It rears back, swinging in my direction, and lashes out, catching me across the shoulder and slashing downward. It feels like a paper cut. She hisses and strikes again, only I'm ready for her. Catching her hand, I pull her toward me and swing her around, letting go long enough for my foot to hit her back and send her flying toward the same wall she put me in. The sickening crack of bone reaches my ears, but I know she's not down. Cass and Nathaniel are fighting with the other one, but it's not my problem.

"What are you?" it hisses and picks itself up off the ground.

"No one knows." I grin and rush her. Her teeth flash in the moonlight, red and ugly. Not the two elongated front teeth you see in movies, just a regular set that's extra sharp.

"We lost Taylor." Robert's voice echoes in my ear. "The three of you need to get out there before the other two are taken out. They're surrounded."

The darkness in me laughs, gleeful to be let out.

Without hesitation, I grab her head and pull with a strength born of demon blood. It comes off easier than I thought it would, and I toss it to the side, going to help Cass and Nathaniel, who have the other one pinned down.

"No, Emma!"

I ignore the sting of teeth as they rip

into me, knowing what's coming.

The dead man's blood takes her down in less than four seconds flat.

Cass moves and severs the head with his blessed blade.

"You look like crap, Hathaway." Eric's voice statics in my ear.

"Think it'll get me out of the Christmas ball on Saturday?"

We both know that's ridiculous and doesn't require an answer.

Cass cleans the blood off his blade using the woman's dress, and then we're moving out of the kitchen and into the hallway leading to the bedrooms.

"Brett, position." Cass waits, but there's no response. We both know he's either dead or he can't speak for fear of giving away his position. "Robert, how many left?"

"Six," Robert answers. "That we know of."

"You got eyes on Brett and his buddy?"

"No."

"This isn't good." Nathaniel checks his gun and switches to thermal vision.

"Nothing in the hallway. I thought you said there were ghosts here."

"I told them to get out."

He shrugs and holds his gun out in front of him like a professional. I wonder how many times he's done this before.

"We clear each room one by one," Cass says, his voice below whisper level. "Don't break formation."

Nathaniel and I nod, following Cass as he moves quietly. The first door we come to is open and empty. One down. The next door is across from the first, and Nathaniel is the one to open it. Empty.

We listen, but the only sound that greets us the beating of our own hearts. Where are they?

The next door is just as empty as the first. The same for the rest of the rooms down here.

Cass points up, and it's the one place I don't want to go.

The memory from that poor nun's dream still hovers at the edge of my mind. The thirst may have lessened, but it hasn't gone away. I don't want it to get worse if I go up there.

But that's where we're going.

At least the steps don't creak, since they're stone.

Once we clear the stairs, I know we're in the right place. I can feel the darkness up here, but it's just the vampires. The blood demon is hiding somewhere outside the church, waiting for its kin to eliminate the threat to their home.

Three rooms upstairs. Six left that we know of.

Three of us, six of them. Odds aren't good.

Cass points to the first door, and Nathaniel opens it. Nothing.

The second door yields one of the creatures. Six silver rounds slow it enough for Cass to swoop in and take its head.

The third door is where we expect them to be.

Shots ring out below, and Robert starts screaming in our ears. He can see what we can't. The ground floor is swarming with vampires. More than he can count.

"Onto the roof!" Cass yells, and we climb out the window and slide along the roof, looking for the lowest access point. Broken bones are a distinct possibility.

Flames shoot out one of the glassless windows on the bottom floor. At least someone down there is still alive.

Nathaniel finds the best spot to jump, and he goes first. Cass is pushing me toward the jumping point when something dark flies overhead. We look up in time to see a pair of large black wings swoop down, knocking Cass aside. Shots ring out, but the bullets bounce off the creature. The same creature from my dreams.

The wings are new. I don't remember seeing them.

It lands on the roof, knowing the boys can't get back up here. There are too many vampires crawling downstairs, daring them to come in.

We hear the shots from their guns, smell the stink of burnt flesh. They're trying to get to me.

But they don't need to. I'd rather be here than my family.

"What are you?" It's the same feminine voice, only a little raspier.

"You speak English now?"

"I learn, adapt."

"You're smart."

She smiles. "Come, child, tell me what you are."

"There's no word to define what I am."

"I smell you. I smell the dark on you, but there's more, there's death and something I can't place."

Eric and Ethan are approaching the church. I can see them out of the corner of my eye.

The creature does too and turns to look at them. She frowns, the grimace curdling her face even more.

"Dead man's blood with a few special herbs."

"Smart."

"Don't go inside, Eric. If any come out, you take them down. Fill them full of silver and take their heads." Cass's order echoes in my ear.

"Roger."

"I'm only replacing the family that was taken from me."

"This is more than the ones still locked in the convent. You've made dozens of them."

She snarls and approaches me. I take several steps backward, but I'm not fast enough. She tackles me, and we go flying off the roof, rolling on the ground.

"Hathaway!"

"Hold your ground!"

The creature grins, blood dripping from its large maw.

I know if I stay here, they don't stand a chance, so I run toward the woods and the swamp, away from my family.

"Hathaway, what are you doing?" Eric's voice is grim.

"What I have to. Now, keep them inside so they can't follow me."

It's eerily like the first dream I had. The land hasn't changed much over the years, especially out here where there's been no development for over a century.

I know it's faster than I am, so I slow down once I reach the edge of the swamp, careful to stay well away from the water. There are gators out here, after all.

I spread out my ghost senses, which only enhances my demonic side. I can smell her. She's close. I creep through the trees, keeping my senses trained on her. A branch snaps to my left, but I don't flinch. I keep going.

"You can't get away from me," she whispers so close I could reach out and touch her. "And you can't kill me either. I'm immortal, child, a creature of darkness."

Her hand grabs hold of me and pulls me against her. "I'm going to be your new mother, little girl."

"I already have three of those, one of which wants me dead. I don't need another one."

She laughs, the sound like silk.

"I'm full of dead man's blood."

"Making you one of mine doesn't require me ingesting your blood. You just have to be empty of it for mine to work."

Her fingernails gouge the inside of my arms, slicing upward. I hiss at the pain and look down to see the blood pouring out of the open veins. She means to let the blood drain and then turn me.

Not today.

I use all the super strength I have to

buck her off. She laughs, and I end up tossed through the air, my back smashing into a tree a few yards away. My entire back is on fire, but I'm able to ignore it and stand.

"Fighting is useless, my child. Just stay still while your body bleeds out."

Its massive bulk blocks out the light of the moon, bathing us in shadows and the smell of the swamp. The mist that normally surrounds the church begins to filter into the woods. The Loa. They're here. The spirits surround me, offering me their strength and wisdom. They make me remember something.

Its only real weakness is the light of day. It's a creature of darkness and death. It creates death.

And I am both dark and light. I am death.

An idea forms, but it may not work. I'm not sure I have enough juice left to make it work even with the Loa's help. The blood loss is starting to get to me.

But I have to try.

"You wanted to know what I was."

"Yes."

"I'm a reaper, so I'm death. I'm part demon, so I am the darkness. But I'm also the daughter of a goddess, so I am the light you hide from."

She hisses and raises her arm to swing down and end me.

It's so easy to find it, nestled there right alongside all my other abilities. I can create life from my blood, but that same blood can take it away.

I catch her arm, my blood smearing on her skin.

And that's when I see what's beneath the mask, as Silas likes to say.

I can see everything about her. I see her creation, her rage, her fear, and her sadness. She grieves the loss of her children like any mother, but she also enjoys the pain she inflicts upon her children and anyone who comes near these grounds.

In the end, she's just another lonely creature, but one who can't stop her own bloodlust.

I open myself up, letting every ability I have flood my body and pour out of my hands and into her. She screams, trying to free herself, but it's useless. More and more light bleeds out of my body and into hers, obliterating every atom, every molecule. I take her apart piece by piece until there's nothing left but a large pile of ash.

It was easy.

And that scares me.

I drop to my knees, suddenly so weak I can barely move. The Loa are still here, and I know I'm not alone. That helps me to focus.

"Eric?"

"Hathaway, where are you?"

"In the swamp. I need..."

I blink, suddenly dizzy, my vision blurring.

"Where in the swamp, Mattie?"

"I..." I take a deep breath. "I need Silas."

And that's the last thing I can manage to say before the blood loss overtakes me.

"Leave it to you to get out of going to the fundraiser," I snark as Mary slips on her stilettos. How she can wear those things is a miracle. I'd fall and break my neck. Her dress, however, is gorgeous and one I wouldn't mind wearing myself. The deep royal blue material makes her eyes stand out. It's not tight, but it does mold to her figure, the skirt part of the dress swaying softly with every movement she makes. Nathaniel is going to have a heart attack when he sees her. My brother has taken quite a liking to Mary. The two of them argue worse than she and Caleb did and that worries me. I'm not sure I want Nathaniel anywhere near Mary.

"I'm injured." I sweep a hand down my chest. "Claw marks, remember? I can't wear that sleeveless dress you picked out for me with claw marks, now, can I?"

"Silas could have healed you."

"He will, *after* the party."

Mary laughs at my smug expression.

"You look beautiful, Mary." Dan is leaning against the doorframe of our bedroom. We're at his apartment, but his bedroom is mine when I'm here so it's ours. I love the way that sounds. Our bedroom.

He's wearing a pair of red plaid pajama bottoms which matches the blue ones I'm wearing. His gray t-shirt fits tightly, showing off his muscles. Dan wasn't ripped before I met him and I loved that version of him, but I like this new version too. We've both changed since that night in the hospital all those years ago. For the better mostly. We've acquired some new fears along the way, but a small dose of fear is healthy for a person. Reminds them they're still alive and they have something left to fight for.

"I really look okay?" Mary checks herself out in the mirror. Her makeup is done to perfection thanks to all those YouTube shows she watches.

"Nathaniel will fall flat on his face."

"Bite your tongue. I'm not worried about how I look because of him."

Dan snorts.

"Really, I'm not."

Dan walks over and pulls her into a hug. "Either way, you're beautiful sister mine. Don't ever forget it." He kisses her on the forehead. "Now go break some hearts and get some of those dodgy old guys to open their wallets and write some checks."

Mary's breath catches when Dan calls her sister. I guess she never knew how much Dan cared about her. I didn't either, but I'm glad he called her sister. It means a lot to both me and Mary.

"Thank you, Dan."

"Your limo is waiting outside. You'd best get going before a certain someone decides to come looking for you."

"I'm not looking for him."

"Mmhmm."

"I'll see you both later, or tomorrow if you're asleep when I get home."

"Go break some hearts, beautiful."

"Don't keep my brother company!" I yell after her retreating back.

"Wasn't planning on it," she calls back.

Dan laughs and then dives on the bed, bouncing us when he lands on it.

"Owwee!"

He's instantly contrite. "Did I hurt you?"

"A little."

"I'm sorry, baby." He rubs his head alongside mine.

"It's okay." I turn into him and wrap myself around him, ignoring the burning in my shoulder and ribs. "I'd rather be here than anywhere else right now."

"You're really glad you got out of that party, aren't you?"

"Did you want to go?"

"God no." He looks horrified at the mere thought. "I hate those things."

"Knock, knock."

We both jump at the sound of Silas's

voice. He's standing where Dan had stood minutes before.

"What are you doing here?" Dan snarls and pulls me closer.

"I came to heal my granddaughter of course. I can't have you reopening those wounds with your carelessness."

Dan growls but I shush him. "He's right. I almost reopened them myself when I took a shower earlier. Besides, it hurts."

Silas grins and comes over, skirting Dan's side and sitting next to me. "You really should have let me do this earlier."

"And be forced into going to the party? Nope."

"I don't know why you dislike parties."

"I don't dislike all parties, just ones put together of snobby rich people."

"Not all of them are snobby." Silas lays his hand on my head and my body begins to fill with warmth. It cascades down my body like a waterfall. I'm warm for the first time in months. Really warm. All the cold from the ghost energy is gone, and nothing is left but the radiating heat of Silas's healing powers.

"Most of them are, and besides, Mary is better at schmoozing than me."

"How are you feeling?" Silas removes his hand and the heat starts to dissipate, but the pain is gone. That's a plus.

"Better. It doesn't hurt now."

"Not your physical injuries, my darling girl. How are *you* feeling?"

"Ahh, well, better. The thirst is gone, at least."

"Thirst?" Dan looks at me curiously.

"Remember the dreams I told you I had? Specifically, the one about the nun being turned?"

Dan nods.

"The tattoo Silas gave me to keep me from experiencing what the ghost did wasn't fixed after the Rougarou attack, so I ended up right there with the nun. When the thirst for blood hit her right before she died, it hit me. When I woke up, I was so thirsty I could have drunk the Mississippi river dry. It stayed with me. It's gone now, but the memory of it isn't. It was awful."

"You didn't tell me, that." He shakes

his head, a rueful smile appearing. "Explains why I drank two entire cases of water."

"Sorry. I forgot to tell you."

"Water's good for you," Silas says and pulls something out of the breast pocket of the suit jacket he's wearing. "I have something for you. An early Christmas present, if you will."

"What is it?" I reach for it, but he holds it back.

"I know you don't remember me from your early years, and maybe one day I can change that, but I thought this might help to show you how much you mean to me." He hands me a rolled-up piece of paper tied with a red ribbon.

Dan leans over to watch me pull the ribbon off and spread the paper out. It's a drawing. In it, there's a Christmas tree with one single present under the tree. Glowing red and blue and orange lights decorate the tree. Standing beside it is a man and a little girl. Above their heads are the names Silas and Me. It's a terrible drawing, attesting to how young I was, but it's proof of what Silas said. I knew it

APRYL BAKER

was true because he's never once lied to me, but seeing this drawing and how much care I put into it…I'm lost for words.

His hand cups my cheek and lifts my face to look at him. "I'm sorry I had to hurt you, Mathilda Louise Hathaway. It's the very last thing I ever wanted to do, but if I didn't, you would have died. I hope one day you realize how much it hurt me to do that to you."

"I told you I forgave you, Silas. And I do. You're my family despite who and what you are. That's all that matters to me. This drawing just proves what I've known for a long time. You love me."

"I do." He looks pained to have admitted that. "It's why I want you to promise me you won't go and get yourself killed."

"I promise to try not to get myself killed."

His nostrils flare at my rewording, but he nods. "That'll do." He leans over and kisses my forehead much as Dan did Mary's. "I have to go, my darling girl. Merry Christmas."

"Merry Christmas, Silas."

He poofs out of the room.

"I thought Caleb demon-proofed the place," Dan says after he's gone.

"Silas gets around the demon-proofing. Even at Zeke's. Drives him crazy."

My finger traces the outline of Silas and me in the painting. This drawing means more to me than anything I've ever gotten. It's a piece of my past, a past where I was loved. "I need to get a frame for this."

"I'll get you one tomorrow." Dan pulls me close again. "You okay?"

"No." A tear leaks out. "I'm not sure I'll ever be okay. I can't remember any of this, Dan. What else don't I remember?"

"I don't know, Mattie, but I promise we'll figure it out together, okay?"

I nod and set the drawing on the bedside table. "Someone did something to me, Dan, and I want to find out who. They took all the protections Rhea gave me away. Maybe that's why I died that day. Maybe they wanted me dead before I ever came into my gifts. They're still out there. Maybe it's the Fallen Angel

Georgina is working for."

"That's a lot of maybes and questions we can't answer tonight. You ready for a surprise?"

"Surprise?"

He gets this devilish look in his eyes and jumps off the bed. Before I can move, he's swept me up in his arms and is carrying me toward the living room.

"Did I ever tell you how much I like your new muscles?"

He laughs and gently sets me down on the couch, pulling a throw off the back and tucking it around me. The lights are off, only the glow from the multicolored lights on the tree giving us any sort of light. The tree is one I picked out for him at Target. The building doesn't allow live trees because of the mess, but the fake tree is just as pretty. We spent the day decorating it yesterday. Well, I supervised, and he and Mary decorated it. Still, it turned out great.

Mary and I also hung stockings on the fireplace, set up a Christmas village on the coffee table, and decorated the rest of the room with Christmas décor. We turned it into a nicer version of our dorm room.

And I love it.

Dan comes back with two packages, one in Santa Claus wrapping paper and one in dark green. They were about the same size. He sets then beside me. "Hands off until I get back."

Pfft. As soon as he's out of sight, I pick them up and shake them. Nether makes a whisper of noise. It's probably clothes, but they don't feel heavy enough. What did he get me?

Dan appears and laughs. "I thought I said not to touch them."

"When have you ever known me to listen to anything?"

"Woman..." He gives me two flute glasses. "Hold these while I pour."

He produces a bottle that looks suspiciously like champagne.

"I thought we could have our own Christmas party. Just the two of us." He opens the bottle and pours the liquid into the glasses. "Sparking grape juice."

He knows I wouldn't have touched the alcohol. This is why I love him. He remembers my little quirks.

"It's not Christmas yet."

"It'll be Christmas Eve in just a few hours. We can cheat." He sits down and raises his glass. "To the new year, which will be filled with love, adventure, and family."

I clink my glass with his. "To the new year."

The bubbles tickle my nose when I take a sip, and I giggle.

He pulls me into his side, and I snuggle close. He smells like oranges, and I wonder what he's been up to.

"Can I ask you something?"

"Sure."

"What happened out there in the woods with the blood demon?"

I sigh. I knew this was coming. We hadn't talked about it at all. I slept for three days after the incident, as I call it. The hunters are going to demand answers too, and I'm not looking forward to that either.

"I was scared, but then I wasn't. The Loa came and lent me their strength. They made me remember her weakness, and I opened myself up to all my gifts, including the ones I got from Rhea, the ones that allowed me to deal with Deleriel. I saw her for what she really was, a creature of darkness, and I knew how to dismantle her. I'm made up of light, and I used that light to burn her to ash. It terrified me how easy it was to stop her, Dan. If the hunters had seen me do it, I'd probably be on their hit list."

"Never gonna happen, baby. They'll have to go through me first."

"They're gonna want answers."

"Then we'll give them answers, just not quite the entire truth. You said the Loa were there. That they helped you."

I nod, not understanding where he was going.

"The Loa helped you, Mattie. Focus on that rather than anything else."

"But how did the Loa help me burn the creature to ash? It was the first of its kind, and that makes it powerful."

"It was also half starved and weakened from having been trapped."

"Are you telling me to lie, Daniel Richards?" I stare up at him,

339

dumbfounded.

"No, Mattie, I'm telling you to stick to the truth, but keep what truth you reveal minimal. Just say the Loa helped you, and you don't remember much because of the blood loss. Which is true. You couldn't even tell us your name when the EMTs asked you."

"I couldn't?"

"You scared Eric and Mary to death."

"What about you? I forgot to ask what happened when I started getting woozy."

"I was home. I'd just gotten off my shift."

"We need to discuss putting limits on what happens to you when this occurs. It might get you killed if you're in a situation where you need all your focus and then you get hit with whatever I am. I don't want to be responsible for your death, Dan."

He's quiet for long minutes, but then he nods. "We'll talk to the demon and see what he can come up with."

Relief floods me, and I hug him tighter. "Thank you."

"Let's open your presents."

I sit up and eagerly reach for them. He snatches them and me the Santa Claus one first. I'm not the girl who gently unwraps things. I tear the paper off and rip the lid open. Inside is a single sheet of paper. Curious, I read what it says without taking it out of the box.

A squeal escapes. "Is this real?"

Dan grins. "It's real, baby, and your father swears he had nothing to do with it. My captain called the lieutenant in charge of Division Four to make them aware of my special talents. I'd talked to her earlier last week about narcotics. I wasn't sure if I was up for it. Not really. It's one thing to work on murders, quite another to go undercover. I passed the detective's exam, but that doesn't mean I felt ready. She told me to stop doubting myself and to suck it up."

I laugh. That sounds about right. His old captain was tougher than most of the men who served under her. She tried to intimidate me once, and that got nowhere. But I respected her for trying, and she respected me for resisting.

"Lieutenant Briggs called me into his

office yesterday to tell me I'd been transferred to his division, effective immediately. Division Four deals with the supernatural crime in the city and technically doesn't exist."

"I'm so happy!" I lunge up and pull his head down to mine, kissing him with all the emotions I can't put into words.

"You'd rather I face monsters than drug dealers?" he asks when I come up for air.

"I'd rather you face monsters all day long instead of twitchy dealers with twitchy gun fingers," I correct him.

"Some of the monsters carry guns too."

"I know that, but chances are you won't run across a gun-toting werewolf faster than you will a dealer who discovers you're a cop or thinks you're one and shoots you just because."

"This really scared you, huh?"

I nod. "More than I can tell you."

"Well, then, now you don't have to worry so much."

"I'm always gonna worry, Dan, because I love you."

"I love you too, baby, and I promise to

be careful."

"That's all I ask."

He leans down and kisses me again, only it's not the same kind of kiss I gave him. This one is deeper, more intimate, and it leaves me breathless when he pulls away.

"You and me, Mattie, we're in it for the long haul."

"We are." I try to kiss him again, and he evades me.

"Uh-uh. You got one more gift to open." He hands me the green box.

Again, I tear it open, only to find a smaller box in the box, with tissue paper packed so tight around it, there was no possibility of it rattling. It's a small black box, and I pull it out carefully.

Dan plucks it out of my hand, and I get nervous. I have a feeling what it is, and I'm not sure if I'm ready, despite what I told him after he'd been shot.

"Remember what I said? In it for the long haul?"

I nod, and he opens the box. Inside lays the most beautiful ring I've ever seen. It's not big, but it's not tiny. You can see the diamond sitting nestled in the ring of silver colored metal. The Christmas tree lights catch the stone, glinting in a myriad of colors. It reflects all the emotions running through me.

"I don't know if you're ready for this yet, so I'm saying it's a promise ring. A promise that one day you and I will get married."

He knows me better than I know myself. He knows I'm terrified of that ring and all the things that come with it. What if I say yes and I lose him? What if something happens to tear us apart? What if…

"Hey." Dan puts the ring down and takes hold of both my hands. "It's okay if you're not ready, baby. I love you, and that ring will go back in my sock drawer. You're all that's important. Not a ring."

But the ring is important to him. It lets him put a claim on me that says to everyone "she's mine." He's gotten very protective since Deleriel, and I think sometimes if he could keep me locked away, he would. He's as scared for me when I'm hunting as I am for him when he's on the job.

But he keeps those fears to himself and loves me. He loves me despite my insecurities, my snarkiness, and my ability to screw everything up.

He loves me despite my being half-demon.

Eli walked away from me when I told him, but Dan stayed. Dan stayed and held me while I cried after Eli left. He told me it didn't matter if I was part demon. He was in it for the long haul.

He's proven that to me so many times.

He loves me despite my own destructive self.

And if I can't give that back to him, I don't deserve the love he gives me every single day.

"Ask me," I tell him in a hushed whisper.

His eyes grow round, and I nod, a small smile tugging at the corners of his lips. He slides off the couch, and while he's not on bended knee, he is on his knees.

"Will you marry me, Mathilda Louise Hathaway?"

"I'll marry you, Officer Dan."

He takes the ring out of the box and slides it on my finger. It looks like an alien sitting there, but it also looks right. The fear and the panic I expected aren't here either. Only a sense of peace. This is right. This is how it's supposed to be, how it was always supposed to be. It just took me a little longer than Dan to get here.

"I love you, Squirt."

And those were the last words spoken for the rest of the night.

ABOUT THE AUTHOR

So who am I? Well, I'm the crazy girl with an imagination that never shuts up. I LOVE scary movies. My friends laugh at me when I scare myself watching them and tell me to stop watching them, but who doesn't love to get scared? I grew up in a small town nestled in the southern mountains of West Virginia where I spent days roaming around in the woods, climbing trees, and causing general mayhem. Nights I would stay up reading Nancy Drew by flashlight under the covers until my parents yelled at me to go to sleep.

Growing up in a small town, I learned a lot of values and morals, I also learned parents have spies everywhere and there's always someone to tell your mama you were seen kissing a particular boy on a particular day just a little too long. So when you get grounded, what is there left to do? Read! My Aunt Jo gave me my first real romance novel. It was a romance titled "Lord Margrave's

Deception." I remember it fondly. But I also learned I had a deep and abiding love of mysteries and anything paranormal. As I grew up, I started to write just that and would entertain my friends with stories featuring them as main characters.

Now, I live Huntersville, NC where I entertain my niece and nephew and watch the cats get teased by the birds and laugh myself silly when they swoop down and then dive back up just out of reach. The cats start yelling something fierce…lol.

I love books, I love writing books, and I love entertaining people with my silly stories.

Facebook:
https://www.facebook.com/authorAprylBaker

Twitter:
https://twitter.com/AprylBaker

Website:
http://www.aprylbaker.com/

Bookbub:
https://www.bookbub.com/authors/apryl-baker

Wattpad:
http://www.wattpad.com/user/AprylBaker7

Newsletter:
https://www.aprylbaker.com/contact

Facebook Fan Page:
https://www.facebook.com/groups/AprylsAngels

Instagram:
https://www.instagram.com/apryl.baker

Blog:
https://www.mycrazycornerblog.com/

Amazon:
https://goo.gl/b1br13

Join our Reader Group on Facebook and don't miss out on meeting our authors and entering epic giveaways!

Limitless Reading

Where reading a book
is your first step to becoming
limitless...

LIMITLESS ◆ PUBLISHING *Reader Group*

Join today! *"Where reading a book is your first step to becoming limitless..."*

https://www.facebook.com/groups/LimitlessReading/